Wayne Frye's *When Jesus Came to Jersey as the Son of Thunder*, *When Jesus Came to Canada to Lead an Indigenous Rebellion in the Broughton Archipelago* and *When Jesus Came to the Black Hills to do the Ghost Dance with the Spirit of Sitting Bull* caused a stir in literary circles, and now he brings the man calling himself Jesus back again. In this harrowing tale, the astonishingly remarkable drifter with the unusual name shows up at a Ladysmith, British Columbia boarding house on beautiful Vancouver Island and once again turns to famous private eye, Aaron Adams, for help in the pursuit of truth and justice. This is a harrowing tale filled with the now famous Frye nuanced commentary on the social ills of society that will have you furiously turning pages in anticipation of what, as usual, will be a mesmerizing surprise ending to a spine-tingling mystery. ------------------*European Library Journal*

Called by one European critic the *Rembrandt of words*, Wayne Frye never fails in delivering a thrilling amalgamation of page-turning excitement in a highly literate work of rip-roaring fiction. This thriller lays bare the hypocrisy that captures far too many people in the web of deceit that passes as religion, while he keeps the reader on the edge of an abyss where the demons of darkness have plans to conjure up evil of the foulest kind. This fourth book in the Jesus series is a fine-tuned mystery that will keep you guessing until the very end. --------------------------*Asian Book Depository*

Images of Ladysmith, British Columbia

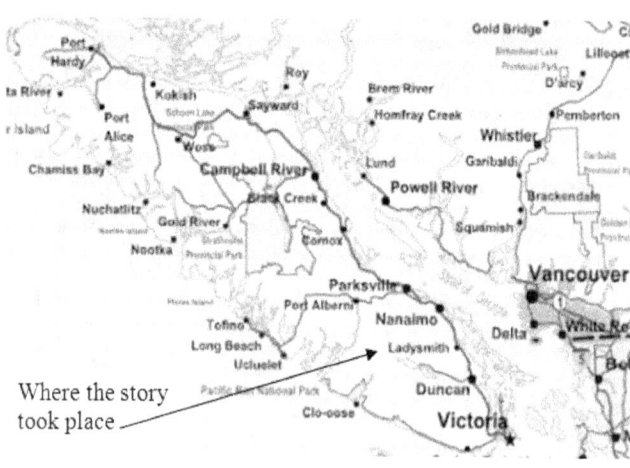

Where the story took place

When Jesus Came
To Ladysmith To Battle
The Angel Of Death

By J. Wayne Frye

#14 in the Aaron Adams Series
#16 in the Lynton Series
#4 in the Jesus Series

This book is written in Canadian English

WHEN JESUS CAME TO LADYSMITH TO BATTLE THE ANGEL OF DEATH

ABOUT THE AUTHOR

Wayne Frye's *Aaron Adams* mysteries, *Chablis Louise Chavez* thrillers, *Girl* books and *Lynton* adventures titillate the brains of those who enjoy tantalizing tales of mystery. His sports book, *How Hockey Saved a Jew from the Holocaust* is required reading in many schools. Growing up in the small town of Asheboro, North Carolina, he wrote his first novel at 15, but waited over twenty years before finally submitting it to a publisher. His life, like the heroes he writes about, has been filled with grand adventure and excitement. He has been a college hockey coach, professor, and at one time, the youngest university president in the USA. Called a marketing genius by the *Los Angeles Times*, he has been a promotional consultant to hockey teams and motion picture companies, and he has been cited for his work with inner-city youths in Los Angeles. A proud Canadian, he lives in Ladysmith, British Columbia on beautiful Vancouver Island.

Some of the over 50 Books by J. Wayne Frye

White Meteors and the Ghost of Sue Ann McGee
Hockey Mania and the Mystery of Nancy Running Elk
Something Evil in the Darkness at Hopkins House
How Hockey Saved a Jew From the Holocaust
The Girl Who Stirred up the Whirlwind
The Girl Who Motivated Murder Most Foul
The Girl Who Said Goodbye for the Last Time
Fall From Apocalypse
Armageddon Now
Worth Part 1: Like a Comet in the Midnight Sky
Worth Part 2: The Night of Thunder Road
When Jesus Came to Jersey as the Son of Thunder
When Jesus Came to Canada to Lead an Indigenous Rebellion
When Jesus Came to the Black Hills to do the Ghost Dance
Lynton Curls Her Hair
Lynton Walks on Water
Lynton and the Vampire at Tagaytay Manor
Lynton Buys a Cell-Phone and Hears the Voice of Doom
Lynton Viñas and Beowulf Perez in the Taal Inferno
Lynton and the Ghosts at the Mansion on Balete Drive
Lynton Viñas: Shadow in the Darkness
Lynton's South African Adventure
Lynton and the Stellenbosch Terror
Lynton and the Cape Town Ghost
Lynton, the Karoo Vampire and the Jewells of Omar Bin Abi
Lynton and the Haunting of the HMS Wind Dancer
Chablis: Avenging Angel for the Forgotten in the City of Lost Hope
Chablis and the Terrorist Who Resurrected the Spirit of Che Guevara
Chablis and Lynton in the Room of Doom
The Rectifier: Dance of Death in the Darkness of Retribution
Pursuit (A Chablis Mystery Primer)
Sammy Sasquatch and the Sts'ailes Star

J. Wayne Frye

WHEN JESUS CAME TO LADYSMITH
TO BATTLE THE ANGEL OF DEATH

TABLE OF CONTENTS

WHEN JESUS CAME TO LADYSMITH
TO BATTLE THE ANGEL OF DEATH

To:
Don Essick, gone but not forgotten.
(What a grand childhood we had!)

And to my daughter, **Andrea** - loved and adored
by so many, and abused by a few because of her
unqualified kindness. Her father's pride in her
knows no boundaries.

And as always to my muse
Lynton Viñas

Catalogue Number: 8341-945-859-2020

ISBN: 978-1-928183-45-7

Fireside Books
Canadian Division - Victoria, British Columbia
Peninsula Publishing Consortium

J. Wayne Frye

WHEN JESUS CAME TO LADYSMITH TO BATTLE THE ANGEL OF DEATH

Prologue
Oppressed by Darkness

The real champions fight a lonely war,
Because their weapons are not bombs and bullets,
But rather, the power of the mind,
The power of righteous indignation,
The power of determination to never
Bow before any tyranny.

The strange looking, thin, bearded man in his thirties strolled up the street which made a steep incline leading to the main part of Ladysmith, British Columbia. He did not seem to gasp for breath as most people around him did, but rather, despite his slight looking frame, appeared to be in excellent physical shape. His strides were

WHEN JESUS CAME TO LADYSMITH
TO BATTLE THE ANGEL OF DEATH

determined with a defiant flair that portended that one had a choice if confronting him; the choice was to show him respect or suffer calamitous circumstances. Yet, there was no animosity in his demeanour, nor any tinge of arrogance. Rather, there was a calmness to him, a calmness that belied the raging distaste he had for vanity and self-righteousness among those who were too quick to point the finger of condemnation.

He was slightly over six feet tall, with long, scraggily chestnut-like hair that flittered about his shoulders with each smooth long measured stride he took. There was determination in his gait, as if nothing could stand in his way. He wore baggy blue jeans and a loose-fitting white cotton shirt that was obviously about two sizes too big. The shirttail hung out over his pants, going halfway to his knees. His brow was barely furrowed, his nose prominent and straight, his chin jutted out. Oh, but the feature that stood out above all others was his eyes. Dark, piercing, almost like beacons, they twinkled with a certain indignation toward the greed he saw way too much in a world where the many poor bowed before the affluent few. He detested the glitziness, the garish display of affluence, the self-absorption displayed by individuals bedecked in fine clothes and glittering jewels that were accentuated by indifference in a world where half of humanity went to bed hungry at the end of the day. The greed of the few subjugated, humiliated and emasculated the many

J. Wayne Frye

to the evils of crony capitalism that utilized propaganda to convince the middle class that it was the poor, not the rich who were the cause of economic hardship.

Moving swiftly up the street, all eyes seemed to be following him, as there was something mystically powerful about this simple man, something that seemed to say this was not a person with whom anyone should trifle. This was a man who by his mere presence seemed to exude authority without having to utter a word.

As the lowering sun reflected off his chestnut hair, there seemed a translucent halo forming around his head, seemingly signalling there was holiness to him. Despite his somewhat unkempt nature, he appeared to be a man of stature, though comely with the aforementioned very determined countenance, such as the beholders might both love and fear him. He had moderately dark skin, appearing to definitely not be of the white race. His forehead was plain and very delicate, his face without spot or wrinkle, beautified with a lovely glow that spoke of a benevolent nature. His nose, as stated, was a bit prominent and his mouth curved slightly to the right through minimally parted lips that made him look innocent but mature. His hands appeared large but delicate.

The streets of the small town of Ladysmith are the most private of public spaces. They are much

WHEN JESUS CAME TO LADYSMITH
TO BATTLE THE ANGEL OF DEATH

the same as walking down a lonely road in a rural place. There is a quaintness to the town that defies description. If you are okay with solitude, if you have matured past the point of loneliness to feel your own worth there is vibrancy to this little piece of paradise on Vancouver Island that can uplift the soul. All around the streets are moments of kindness, fleeting smiles and gestures of appreciation that are the beauty on this canvas of weathered grey by the bay. Still, within this quaint place are dark corners inhabited by those who refuse to offer the light of optimism to people lost in the vicious cycle of life, where the struggle for survival makes confidence tumble down a mountain of lost hope like an avalanche. These were the people this man, who had just come to Vancouver Island from a recent sojourn in the storied Black Hills of South Dakota, was concerned with, because he always extended a hand up to those felled by the misery of every day life faced by those who had to toil in obscurity.

This day, as he looked about the small town while swiftly moving toward his destination, he noticed a rhythm to the feet on the streets, a chaotic rhythm born of the universal soul of mankind. There was a tempo to it all, an upbeat pitch asking why the strollers were not actually dancing instead of taking their usual uneventful steps. So in his imagination, songs dialled up their volume and he saw a musical of sorts. The bright umbrellas some were carrying in anticipation of

J. Wayne Frye

WHEN JESUS CAME TO LADYSMITH
TO BATTLE THE ANGEL OF DEATH

rain were now twirling in the late day sunlight and strangers to him seemed to be feeling an exuberance to be in such a beautiful place; although, he sensed many were carrying heavy burdens. It was as if the streets were a set for a movie, and all about him were actors for better and worse, actors in the mosaic of life. Ironically, all about him he could see no buildings with any cracks and no peeling paint, because a movie had recently been filmed on the streets, and the movie company had repainted all the downtown buildings on the main street to make them appear spotless. Unfortunately, this man knew that appearances could often be incredibly deceiving. No matter how wonderful the place seemed on the exterior, there were deep, dark blemishes that could not be seen by the naked eye. Those blemishes were what made life so unbearable for people in a world where want was the norm for the many because of the greed of the few.

The streets, on the top, seemed almost perfect with sleek new surfaces that were once greyed by the bleaching of the sun. The road that was once a monochrome patchwork now appeared fresh and vibrant. However, despite these fixes, there were still cracks underneath hidden from view that would one day pop through the surface and require patching again. The trees that were once fine saplings with soft foliage were now gnarled, growing tall but without strength. This, unfortunately, was the real world, where underneath there was weakness of mind, body and spirit. The barks of the trees were mossy from the perennial dampness and incessant rain that poured out a special kind of misery reserved for those caught in the perpetual winter of discontent. The sidewalk, for the most part, was still smooth concrete, albeit scattered with debris from the moulting trees that were preparing for winter.

It always depressed this man to see that the parity of opportunity and hope, even in a great nation like Canada, was elusive. What a discouraging place the world was for the majority who were expected to toil for minimum wages, while those at the top of the economic ladder lived lives of splendorous excess with money accumulated on the backs of the less fortunate. He longed in his kind, caring heart for a new and better order of society where there would be neither rich nor poor, where all would have meaningful work with a truly living wage. Not just a handful of rich people would enjoy the grandeur of a life free of want, but all the hard working people who toiled in obscurity might enjoy the fruits of their common labour. He longed for machines and other improvements to ease the work of all and not to enable a select few to grow fabulously rich at the expense of billions upon billions of poor people who, by virtue of their lineage, were not part of the privileged class that garnered the means of production through inheritance, not hard work.

J. Wayne Frye

WHEN JESUS CAME TO LADYSMITH
TO BATTLE THE ANGEL OF DEATH

Turning right off First Avenue, the stranger began the steep ascent up Roberts Street. A red letter box stood as if on sentry duty, guarding the wide street that was filled with old miners' homes from the turn of the century when Ladysmith was made an instant town by a coal baron who moved houses from a nearby coal mining village to provide accommodations for the slave-wage workers who made him rich. The small houses were deep and narrow with long forgotten gardens stretching behind them, gardens where the worn and weary workers, despite having employment, were forced to grow some of their own food in order to put sustenance on often bare tables.

Jesus was a man who knew privation, ridicule, hardship and indigence, because he continually walked a precipitous and difficult path that put him at odds with the authorities, with those who protected the privileged while degrading the poor. He was a man with many enemies who saw him as a danger to their privileged status, and yet, he never cowered in fear, never wavered in his dedication to the righteous cause of equality of opportunity for which he fought. Despite being under constant fire from an enemy with the superior weapons of privilege, he never retreated, never raised his hands in surrender and never gave up on the search for justice.

As the lengthened shadows of the ending day melted away into the coming twilight, the streetlamps with their bowed graceful necks stood tall waiting to flicker on to greet the night. They would also greet this stranger, this man who had walked so far and so long and to so many places to offer wise counsel and be a true saviour to those who were oppressed by darkness.

WHEN JESUS CAME TO LADYSMITH
TO BATTLE THE ANGEL OF DEATH

Chapter 1
A Cesspool of Ignorance

You cannot push truth off a cliff.
You may, of course, ask why?
Well, it is simple.
You see; truth can fly!

The Dunsmuir Lodge dates back to the days when coal baron, James Dunsmuir, stood on the present site of the town and said like Brigham Young when he arrived in the Salt Lake Valley of Utah in the USA, "This is the place." It was on the side of the hill that he demanded his workers build an elaborate structure that he deemed be called the Dunsmuir Lodge, and it was there that the elite of that day and age gathered regularly.

WHEN JESUS CAME TO LADYSMITH
TO BATTLE THE ANGEL OF DEATH

Years later, when the famed French Maestro, Maurice Ravel, came to Ladysmith after conducting an orchestra in the British Columbia capitol of Victoria and was made an honorary member of the club, he said, as he signed the lodge register, "I would rather see my name on that than on the marquee of the Vienna Opera House." Now, in the present day, the club was no longer such a prestigious place, but it still carried a certain mystique to it, a sense that only the elite of the area were allowed to belong.

On the very night that the walking man mentioned in the prologue arrived in town, there were only five people in the club dinning hall, four of them busy with dinner and one reading in front of the fireplace. They were on the second floor of the building. There is only one long table in the dining room of the club, and at the far end of the room the fire was glowing red hot despite it being relatively mild that day, and to the right of the fireplace there was a broad bow window of diamond panes, which looked out upon the street. Four of the five men there that very late afternoon were regular members but the stranger reading a paper by the fire was not known to be a member. The assumption was that he was a guest waiting for a sponsoring member to show up.

Over the years, the club had hit on hard times and had admitted people of more modest means to keep up club finances, as the Dunsmuir

J. Wayne Frye

endowment for the club had long ago been exhausted, along with the desire of most people to belong to a club that had outlived the idea of a defined aristocracy. Still, there were the few who felt belonging to the club somehow made them special.

The four men at the table pulled at the bones on their barbecued rib dinners and sipped their Scotch and sodas, while they conversed with such charming animation that a visitor to the club, which does not generally tolerate visitors, would have thought them probably equally at home at the country club in the nearby city of Nanaimo.

The men, munching on their meals, watched as the person by the fireplace got up and strolled over to the window. He was an older man in his sixties with the apparent intensity of wisdom. One who was, no doubt, a deep thinker. His grey hair, his broad shoulders, his mildly muscular body, his strong jaw line, his dark intense eyes, his Romanesque nose all congealed into a uniqueness of character almost as interesting as the man walking up the street outside the club.

There was a calm quietness that permeated his being. It was a calm so vibrant that it spread like a plague of respect and awe among those who observed him walking over to the window as if he was a man of destiny moving toward a reckoning that would make the earth quake with his resolve.

WHEN JESUS CAME TO LADYSMITH
TO BATTLE THE ANGEL OF DEATH

It reached out of his head and enfolded him in its bold arms, sent its stealthy, suckered tentacles inching along the insides of his skull, hovering the knolls and dells of his ageing swarthy body, dislodging old sentences, whisking them off the tip of his silver-tipped tongue that surely said little, but when anything was said, it was done with intensity. The man, looking out across the street, said, as he astonishingly observed his old friend, whom he had not seen for over two years walking by, "What a strange person. He dresses like a pauper, but he has the stride and the manner of an affluent aristocrat. There is something remarkable about him. I know that man, and I know from experience that where he goes trouble follows. He has brought down economic and political rulers from their thrones and raised up the humble and meek. He has filled the hungry and lost with nourishment of the soul and sent the arrogant rich cowering in fear. He breaks unjust laws, because he sees them as a way of coddling the rich and powerful. He interprets the police as often being promoters of unjustness in service to the privileged class. He has been in prisons and turned those prisons into rebellious dens of the afflicted who will not tolerate inhumane conditions. He cavorts with rebel-rousers, the malcontents of a world where greed rules with impunity. That is a man to be feared, and to be respected for his refusal to tolerate oppression, prejudice or inequity of any kind. I think of myself as a strong man, but I quiver in his presence."

J. Wayne Frye

WHEN JESUS CAME TO LADYSMITH
TO BATTLE THE ANGEL OF DEATH

The men at the table stared out the window at the tall, thin man with long flowing chestnut hair gracefully gliding up the street. All there were mesmerized by the countenance he displayed. They were speechless, but they needed no words to indicate they were overwhelmed by the man's presence and manner just as was the man who had been sitting quietly by the fireplace and was now staring out the huge bowed window.

One man, between bites of his barbecued ribs, said, "So, you know this loathsome looking creature, then?"

He replied, "That is a man of great daring in an era when the days for romantic adventure and deeds of daring have passed, and the fault lies with people like you four who have become complacent in accepting a 9 to 5 routine where you are nothing but robotic caricatures who are slaves to the corporate bottom line. You can see in that man an aura, a light of freedom that shines through the darkness of lost hope that engulfs the entire world in the evil of greed. That singular man is the embodiment of what I wish I could be. He bows before no one; he is not one to be trifled with. He shows with each long smooth determined stride great boldness, courage, conviction and fearlessness. That, my friends, is a real man."

Taken aback by the boldness of this stranger among them, the four there were overcome with silence. They were unable to reply to the rebuke given them, as the man continued, "Believe me, I will do all I can to avoid that man down there, because I know he will stir up trouble in this quaint little town. He never goes anywhere without purpose, and his purpose always is based upon his intense hatred of seven things that are an abomination to him: haughty eyes of evil, a lying tongue, hands that shed innocent blood, a heart that devises wicked plans, feet that make haste to run to evil, a false witness who breathes out lies and one who sows discord among people. He does not wrestle against flesh and blood, but against the rule of the corrupt, against the unscrupulous authorities, against the economic powers that exploit the darkness of greed. He rails against the nefarious, debauched forces of evil that sow a harvest of treachery."

The man took a deep breath and shook his head as he walked back to the fireplace and eased back into his chair. Inside, his blood was racing through his veins like a river over a steep waterfall; because he had not come to Ladysmith to meet up with the man he had shared three previous adventures with, adventures that had tried his soul. Adventures that had made him face the fact that there was one man in the entire world who truly was as close to holy as any he had seen in his 63 years on earth. Yes, it was this very man he had seen striding up the street outside the club window.

J. Wayne Frye

WHEN JESUS CAME TO LADYSMITH
TO BATTLE THE ANGEL OF DEATH

As he sat there in the chair, staring toward the door at the back of the room, the others were at the table enjoying the ribs but they could not get the man by the fireplace off their minds, because he had touched them harshly with his words, touched them in a way that made each one of them examine their lot in life, their place in a world where they were part of the many who were obsessed with trying to impress others and did not realize that they had no depth to their being, no real accomplishments other than economic gold in a mine that was dark without a glimmer of light seeping into their souls. These people lived in darkness and did not even know it, and that man outside walking up the street could see into people's souls, see into the blackness that surrounded those who judged their worth by the content of a bank account rather than the content of character.

This man in the club was completely unknown until someone came to the door and called out to him, "Mr. Adams, they will see you now. Please follow me."

As he sprang to his feet, he said, "Just call me Aaron."

The men at the table, for a long time said nothing. They kept as still as a stone. They hardly seemed to be breathing at all. When at last one began to speak, it sounded almost as though he

WHEN JESUS CAME TO LADYSMITH
TO BATTLE THE ANGEL OF DEATH

was singing a reverent hymn, when he said, "I be damned! I can't believe who that was. That was Aaron Adams! He was made famous by the writer, Wayne Frye, who lives right here in Ladysmith."

How does one properly describe the mystique of Aaron Adams, the private detective glorified by Wayne Frye, the author who actually called Ladysmith home, where he wove tales of intrigue and adventure about the man who many called the icon of iconoclastic independence, the man with the barbed-wire soul who could slay malfeasant malcontents with a mere stare of indignation. Yes, it was Aaron Adams, a tough guy's tough guy, a hard man but with a depth of compassion for the downtrodden - those stomped on by the evil of economic inequity and the cold hearted callousness of hypocrisy.

He had moved toward the door like Will Kane when he strode onto the street in the movie *High Noon* ready to face overwhelming odds unafraid of anything that might stand in the way of the justice he was about to mete out. Aaron Adams was every bit as fearless as Will Kane. He had proven himself time after time, and had no fear of death, no fear of any man, because he had a confidence that elevated him into a mountain of stone in the face of adversity. Yet, Aaron was tough only when he had to be, tender when he should be. He was no predator, because he didn't have to prove himself. Guys who have to pretend to be tough, they aren't, but Aaron never pretended to be tough. He was!

As he walked through the doorway, the men at the table had stopped chomping on their ribs, because every one of them was in awe of the presence of a legend, a legend that had come to Ladysmith and was right there in the Dunsmuir Lodge. One of the men said, "Damn, we been talked to by the legend. I once met Wayne Frye, and he told me when I asked about Aaron Adams that his books were part fiction and part reality, but that if I ever met the real Aaron Adams I would shiver in my shoes. Well boys, I am shivering."

Aaron walked into the smoking room, which was no longer a smoking room by virtue of a more sane policy, but was now a private den for special meetings arranged by members. Aaron stood before five men with his iconic grin that seemed to say, "Let me hear it, gentleman."

One man, sitting in a recliner that was not reclined stood up and said, as he extended his hand, "A pleasure Mr. Adams. I have heard much about you."

The man, Stanley Chemer, was a cartographer by trade, a dying profession in the days of computers, but his age and station in life assured he had nothing to worry about. He made maps, because he had been an intrepid traveller of the world who used the profession of cartographer as pretence to travel and, as a result of it being a business, was able to make all his extravagant vacations, lavish accommodations and gourmet meals tax deductible. That was par for the course when it came to the wealthy. They always were able to take advantage of the tax man, while the average "Joe" could not deduct lavish living from his taxes. He even liked to brag about the dangers of his profession, and how he had to face constant trials and tribulations, but the presence of danger does not constitute adventure. If that was so, the chemist who studies high explosives, or who investigates deadly poisons passes through adventures daily. No, adventures are for the adventurous, and true adventure had died long ago from inertia in dear old Chemer.

The men in the room had no true sense of adventure, because their lives were ones of inherited position and the corresponding resplendent pleasures of privilege as a result of class distinctions that they somehow thought made them special in the grand scheme of things. In reality, they were leeches who lived lives of excess while drawing down trust funds. Their sense of adventure was more likely to revolve around weighty matters like spilled Burgundy on a gentleman's expensive coat sleeve as a result of a poorly trained waiter who did not realize the proper way to serve the elite.

WHEN JESUS CAME TO LADYSMITH
TO BATTLE THE ANGEL OF DEATH

The other men there rose and introduced themselves to Aaron. However, one of them at the far side of the fireplace did not budge from his seat. He was an elderly and somewhat portly person, with a sternly wrinkled countenance. He wore continually a disdainful smile of arrogant confidence and ill-nature. It was a face which looked familiar to Aaron, but he could not place it. The man held a book from him at arm's-length, as if to adjust his eyesight, and his brows were knit with up-turned disinterest. He looked the kind of fellow who, by station in life, thought he was above the law, above using common niceties to anyone beneath his exalted station of privilege, above having to exhibit any standards of courtesy to those of a lesser social status. Aaron could easily image if someone riled his sensibilities that in days of old he would have had them bound and gagged and thrown into a chair while the passers-by peons would take to their heels, as his hired bullies and ruffians would convey to the man through violence the futility of offending someone of the upper class. First impressions can, of course, be deceiving, and the usually astutely accurate observations of Aaron would prove, at least for the time being, erroneous.

Purposefully ignoring the man who remained seated, Aaron took a seat and said, "I am here because I am not in the habit of turning down a $10,000 retainer check along with a First Class plane ticket. Of course, my biographer, Wayne

WHEN JESUS CAME TO LADYSMITH
TO BATTLE THE ANGEL OF DEATH

Frye, lives here and I have not seen him in some time, so it seemed apropos to at least see what I could do for you gentleman. Now, perhaps you could tell me why you think it worth $10,000 just to have me come here for a chat."

The man reading shrugged his shoulders as if to say, "This is not my idea."

As the other gentlemen took seats, the youngest among them said, "And why Mr. Adams do we want you for this little adventure?"

"Indeed," replied Aaron.

Pointing at the portly man who was still reading his book, Stanley Chemer said, "That is our MPP (Member of Provincial Parliament), and in a day or so he is going to vote for a bill that will raise taxes on those who make more than $200,000 a year. It is an NDP (New Democratic Party) government measure, and he is at the point in assuring its passage, and so big is his following and his influence that it will garner wide spread support. Now, had I the spirit of my ancestors I would bring chloroform from the nearest pharmacy and drug him in that chair. I would tumble his unconscious form into a cab, and hold him prisoner until after the vote. If I did, I would save the rich great consternation and worry on how they could afford to continue the support of the poor malcontents who refuse to work."

WHEN JESUS CAME TO LADYSMITH
TO BATTLE THE ANGEL OF DEATH

Aaron eased back in his chair and surveyed those around him with some repugnance, and also looked at the portly gentleman by the fireplace and realized you could misjudge someone based on appearance, because although he was obviously of the privileged class, he was the one among the people there, who, being a New Democrat, was partial to working men and women.

Still, the man had not lifted his eyes from the book he was diligently reading, seemingly totally disinterested in the conversation. He appeared engrossed in the book, but it was obvious that he was also listening.

"To look at him now," Stanley Chemer said, "one would not guess he was deeply concerned with what we are about to convey to you."

The others nodded silently, as Chemer continued. "He has not lifted his eyes from that book since we first entered. His silence speaks volumes on the matter at hand."

"Oh, yes, he will speak," muttered the youngest among them moodily. "During the last hours of debate in Parliament, he will rise and eloquently talk of how the less fortunate among us are set upon by the wealthy and made to subsidize their lavish living, their splendorous excesses that suck the life out of humanity. He will deplore the affluent whom he says callously disregard the welfare of the lesser among us. This is what keeps the NDP in power. They depend on the riff-raff of society to support them, and in turn, the riff raff expect the NDP to provide handouts."

Aaron rose from his chair, riled by the apparent disrespect paid to the working men and women, whom he always championed. He reached into his breast coat pocket and took out the check for $10,000 and tossed it on the coffee table. He was not a man who minced words. "Gentlemen, and I use the word negatively in your cases, let me make something clear. I am at the stage of my life, both philosophically and economically, where I do not suffer fools lightly, nor do I accept arrogance from those born into privilege. I have more respect for a janitor than a C.E.O. I have more respect for someone who asks me if I want fries with my hamburger than someone who cruises the bay in a yacht. I have more respect for a person who, with a gun, steals a pizza to fill an empty belly than I do a banker who steals from widows and orphans with the stroke of a pen. I am too polite to use the vulgar term for what you are, but you know the term, and you all fit it perfectly."

The old man put down his book and started applauding. Smiling, he said, "Touché."

Chemer grimaced and said, "Believe me, Mr. Adams; you have gotten on Porter's good side with that little tirade. The weighty work in which the eminent statesman is so deeply engrossed is called *The Disappearance* – one of your cases so ably told by Dr. Wayne Frye of Ladysmith. No doubt you have read and lived it. It supports the contention about us you just made."

"Actually, Wayne is not my favourite writer," offered a sullen Aaron. "I am actually more the Hemingway type. For an MP, I'd say Wayne's novels might be disconcerting if you don't like some politics with your literature, as he has some pretty profound things to say about the lack of compassion from politicians. "

The MP, his face like a piece of slightly yellowed ivory, his high white forehead knotted fiercely with wrinkles, his mouth like a thin knife, his smile like the flicker of light across a razor-sharp blade, his determination like a serrated slicer that could cut through bone, eased forward in his chair. There was but a slight flicker of light in the delicate but fierce stare to his eyes. And when he sniffed a deep breath with sharp and private concentration through his long, pointed nose with a countenance that was crinkled and crisp as lettuce, it was obvious this was a man who harboured deep thoughts.

He said, "I am Charles Porter, and believe me, Wayne's novels are an acquired taste, and they do deliver some pretty devastating blows to politicians. His books are actually a vice. It is dissipation I suppose, but I am addicted. I am noted for reading Frye's works, as I quote him often in Parliament, or maybe I am quoting you and just don't know it, as there is a fine line between the fiction Frye writes and the reality lived by the famous Aaron Adams. I tell you nothing can tear me from one of his tales of murder, robbery and evil chicanery. Back when there was a train between Nanaimo and the Parliament in Victoria, I often would miss my stop in Ladysmith, because I was so absorbed in one of his books. His *Armageddon Now* still makes me tremble that a terrorist can be a hero. Now that book laid it out plain and simple, exposed all the evil arrogance and hypocrisy of that country south of here that went over the edge to use terrorism to fight terrorism. I still, on occasion, contact the World Court in The Hague to ask why they have not prosecuted Bush and Cheney for war crimes. Of course, the USA doesn't belong to the World Court for that very reason. They fear justice!"

Aaron, nodding in agreement, said, "I think you and I are on the same wave length."

Porter looked down at the check on the table and said, "Don't be so quick to toss away a pot full of money. My friends, or maybe I should say my make-believe friends, because I am sure none of them vote for me, may be a bit overbearing, but that is because they have not been taught compassion for the less fortunate. They are trust funders who think by virtue of birth to the privileged class that they are somehow entitled to look down on those who toil for their sustenance."

"Well, I hope Mr. Porter that you are the exception rather than the rule when it comes to politicians. However, I am afraid that there are few exceptions. I am an old man now, and I no longer have any tolerance for wasting time, and I believe that sending that check was a way to appeal to the greed that motivates most people, which, frankly, has never been a part of my makeup. I am not rich in money, but I am rich in integrity. I have turned down a lot of money over the years, and my bank account reflects a lack of greed, but an abundance of integrity."

"Well put, Mr. Adams," offered Porter.

The eyes of all were fastened upon Porter, and each saw with great fascination that with his forefinger he was now meticulously separating the last two pages of the book. The Member of Parliament struck the table softly with his open palm. "This is an intriguing story called the *Disappearance*, and it fascinates me Mr. Adams that it is based on fact, based on one of your many exploits that have been chronicled by Wayne Frye. It is incredible how so many unbelievable adventures have fallen into your lap. I must admit that I believe the stories are filled with monumental embellishments."

WHEN JESUS CAME TO LADYSMITH
TO BATTLE THE ANGEL OF DEATH

"You are right Mr. Porter," replied an unapologetic Aaron, "Wayne has perhaps made things seem more exciting than they were, because detective work is not all guts, guns and glory. It is a methodical following of clues and meticulous research into what makes people do the things they do, things that emanate from the dark side."

Porter, separating the last two pages without looking at them, but rather gazing directly at Aaron, said, "Ah, the dark side? Yes, there is plenty of that."

"You see," offered Aaron, "Wayne is able to comprehend what most others don't. He can identify hypocrisy better than anyone I have ever known. He calls out those of faith who bow before Jesus but only do lip service to what he proclaimed. He abhors the finger-pointing of the self-righteous who tell others how to live, but do not practice what they preach. He sees the evil of the capitalist system that has trapped 99% of the world in service to the 1% who truly control everything. He may embellish, but he does, believe me, get the true nature of who I am. I am a tough guy, yes, but I am tough against the same hypocrisy he deplores. I am tough against the privileged class that gets preferential treatment. I stand with determination against the evil of those who prey upon the downtrodden, the poor, the afflicted, the forgotten millions who toil in obscurity for their daily bread. I am an avenger for justice that is sorely lacking in a world where a person's value is based upon the size of their bank account rather than the size of their character. We live in a sick world, Mr. Porter, and I am the doctor on call sometimes who is dedicated to curing some of that sickness in my own small way, a way that often requires radical measures, extremely radical measures."

Aaron, enjoying the banter with Mr. Porter, could see that he was taking it all in with an intensity of purpose. He observed Aaron with sharp precision, as though the words bore to him some special application. He was still fingering the last two pages of his book as though trying to decide whether to finish it or continue his discussion with Aaron. He looked up from the book and said, "The private eye is uniquely American isn't he? We don't really have that sort of character in Canada."

Aaron replied, "The P.I. story is linked with the western story, the one that has the loner riding into town to take on the bad guys single-handedly. The reason the P.I. has to do it single-handedly is because most people are willing to wear their balls and chains just to survive. I am not one of those people. I live by a code that says that the guilty, in most cases, because there are some exceptions, must be punished, and if there is no one else willing to stand up for justice, then I am! I particularly insist that people of privilege should be held to the same standards as those who are not affluent. I insist that the colour of your skin should not determine the amount of justice to which you are entitled. I see the police, far too often, being used to safeguard the rich from the poor. The world has never moved beyond the feudal system where the Lords of the Manor control the lives of the peasants. Today, the Lords of the Manor are the corporation C.E.O.'s who sit in their palaces of excess and are never satisfied with what they have. They must always have more and more, and they get more on the backs of the working men and women they exploit."

Porter looked down and read, seeming to ignore Aaron to the point that Aaron turned and started to leave. Porter slammed the book closed and said, "Typical Frye surprise ending. Damn, it grabs you right in the gut. Did it really happen that way?"

Turning back to Porter, Aaron said, "Wayne has found the real character of what he sometimes calls the lonely profession. It is solitary, often horribly lonely and very often dangerous both physically and emotionally; it is the film noir of the real world. So, yes, it did happen that way. His books are like life, extremely unpredictable and often with gruelling intensity."

Porter took a deep breath and said, "That is why you have been selected, because you live up to what Raymond Chandler, the creator of Philip

WHEN JESUS CAME TO LADYSMITH
TO BATTLE THE ANGEL OF DEATH

Marlow, called the creed of character that is necessary in a man who chooses what you coin the lonely profession. In everything that can be called art there is a quality of redemption. It may be pure tragedy and high tragedy, and it may be pity and irony, and it may be the raucous laughter of the strong man. But down mean streets a man must go who is not himself mean, who is neither tarnished nor afraid. The sanctified private detective must be such a man. He is the hero; he is everything. He must be a complete man and a common man and yet an unusual man. He must be, to use a rather weathered phrase, a man of honour by instinct, by inevitability, without thought of it, and certainly without saying it. He must be the best man in his world and a good enough man for any world. I do not care much about his private life; he is neither a eunuch nor a satyr. I think he might seduce a queen, but I am quite sure he would not spoil a virgin, because if he is a man of honour in one thing, he is a man of honour in all things. He is a relatively poor man, or he would not be a detective at all. He is a common man or he could not go among common people. He has a sense of character, or he would not know his job. He will take no man's money dishonestly and no man's insolence without a due and dispassionate response. He is a lonely man and his pride demands that you will treat him as a proud man or be very sorry you ever saw him. He talks as the man of character talks, with a rude wit, a lively sense of the grotesque, a disgust for sham and a contempt for pettiness. As I have read about you in Wayne Frye's books, I see a story of a man who searches for the hidden truth, and who has a keen sense of adventure. He has a range of awareness that startles, but it belongs to him by right, because it belongs to the world he lives in. If there were enough like him, the world would be a very safe place to live in, without becoming too dull to be worth living in. You are the man we need!"

Aaron, stunned by the eloquence of Porter, again took his seat, looked down at the $10,000 check, then up at Porter and said, "Maybe you should be a writer, Mr. Porter. You certainly have learned a lot from Wayne, and no doubt, from Raymond Chandler when it comes to turning a phrase. I am afraid even Wayne knows that I prefer Raymond Chandler's prose to his. Who can turn a better phrase than Chandler did as you said when he commented that down these mean streets a man must go who is not himself mean, but who is neither tarnished nor afraid. I, Mr. Porter, am tarnished and sometimes maybe even a little afraid, but I am never surprised at the cruelty of which man is capable, nor am I surprised by my own determination to never bow before the privileged class that rules with relative impunity. I have seen the evil of those who, in their absurdly garish display of arrogance, look about as economically inconspicuous as a tarantula on a slice of angel food cake. While people live in cardboard boxes in America, the arrogant privileged class ride by in their chauffeured limousines, but they will one day, I sincerely hope, find that there is no trap so deadly as the trap you set for yourself. The arrogant rich are building the guillotine that will slice their greed into oblivion one day."

"You should have been a writer yourself, Mr. Adams. You know how to turn a very nice phrase," replied Porter.

"Maybe one day, who knows?" offered Aaron. "But the thrill of the chase is hard to put aside. However, I see you are a man who enjoys the vicarious chase through reading. Reading, in today's world, is a lost art I am afraid."

Porter replied. "Reading is one of the absolute greatest acts of civilization, because it takes the free raw material of the mind and builds castles of possibilities. Unfortunately, in today's world, reading has certainly become a lost art. Reading is to the mind what exercise is to the body, but just like a person who refuses to exercise and gets flabby, refusing to read makes the mind flabby. The reason politics is filled with miscreants who are not held accountable is because people simply refuse to read the truth about how they are being raped by their own ignorance. Rather than read, they absorb the pabulum fed them by popular media. It is easier to let someone else do their thinking for them. They are more interested in

WHEN JESUS CAME TO LADYSMITH
TO BATTLE THE ANGEL OF DEATH

America's Got Talent, where a cue card is held up to tell the audience when to applaud so that the viewers can be manipulated into thinking someone with no talent is talented. They laugh at jokes which are so ridiculously unfunny that a laugh track must be inserted so the viewers believe what is not funny is funny. What thinking person would truly care what a pack of rich, privileged morons like the Kardashians are up to? The world has become a cesspool of ignorance."

J. Wayne Frye

WHEN JESUS CAME TO LADYSMITH
TO BATTLE THE ANGEL OF DEATH

Chapter 2
Her Cold Heart Had Melted

One song can spark a moment.
One whisper can ease pain.
One tree can start a forest.
One bird can herald spring.

One smile begins a friendship.
One look can show affection.
One star can guide a ship at sea.
One word can overcome addiction.

One vote can change a nation.
One sunbeam can light a room.
One candle can wipe out darkness.
One laugh can conquer gloom.

J. Wayne Frye 39

WHEN JESUS CAME TO LADYSMITH
TO BATTLE THE ANGEL OF DEATH

One step can start a journey.
One touch can end fear.
One hope can raise the spirit.
One kind act can show you care.

One voice can speak with wisdom.
One heart can know what's true.
One life can make a difference.
One stranger can deliver what's due.

The man who had walked by the window as Aaron looked out upon the main street of Ladysmith, having turned to his right, was now making his way up the steep incline of Roberts Street, when about half way up he looked to his right at what was once a church. It had been converted into a boarding house. The man stopped in front of it and stared long and hard at the cross that was still on top of the steeple.

Looking at that cross sent a chill up the man's spine, because he saw it as a symbol of cruelty that makes God out to be a vengeful, homicidal deity who can be satisfied only with the death of his son in atonement for the sins of all regardless of how kind and caring many were, sins that were defined as trapping every man and woman in the pit of hopeless cowering before an all-powerful God who would mete out vengeance on the innocent as well as the guilty. He felt the doctrine of blood atonement was an outmoded product of power, injustice and terrorism which made the cross a sign of conquest rather than love that should shape Christian identity. Like the money changers in the temple, this man saw ecclesiastical might as sanctioned cruelty that was embraced by those who got some kind of perverse pleasure in finger-pointing hypocrisy.

The man looked at the cross with a palpitating heart and tears in his eyes. He could feel the pain inflicted by those who nailed a man to the cross in subservience to unbridled authority; just as so many continued to bow to the authority in the present day, an authority that served the interests of the few at the expense of the many. He thought the symbol of love would be more appropriately displayed by a woman holding a newborn child as it suckled on her breast. Oh, but that would be an abomination to so many who rant against the sins of the flesh by ascribing a baby suckling in a mother's arms to sexualization. This was the method of those who were always ready to condemn and ridicule rather than practice the magnanimous love and nonjudgmental acceptance exemplified by a man named Jesus Christ.

The ill spirit of the former church was apparent, as the man knew that there was something sleeping in the walls of the dilapidated building, something that had hidden itself in darkness by retreating into the welcoming wood away from the dust of the past when a minister had stood in his pulpit and raged against sin, raged against permissiveness, raged against those who defied his definition of righteousness. He had been a stern master of God's word, but it was a perverted word he delivered every Sunday morning, perverted by his adherence to the idea of the vengeful God of the Old Testament. It stayed there in this place with the lost memories of hugs and laughter that were deplored as machinations of the devil portrayed by a man in the pulpit who knew not the magnanimity of forgiveness, but rather embraced the finger-pointing hypocrisy that had no representation of the real Jesus who looked upon judgementalism as a harbinger of evil manifested in the hearts of those who sat on thrones of arrogance. The front porch, with the peeling paint flakes and dirt of neglect on the paint bare timbres, circled what was once the sanctuary. It appeared desperately in need of loving care, as the outdoor furniture lay still without the warmth and sense of family.

He steadily moved toward the steps and walked up to the door without trepidation, ignoring the ill-looking nature of a place that despite being surrounded by other homes appeared to harbour a fondness for isolation within the walls that made the building almost shiver. It was as if the building often shut every door and window to the outside world, hoping to be invisible, hoping to hide the pain inside the walls that stood against the outside world. The building appeared to have chosen solitude for itself, as if harmony was a luxury it could forgo. The house shuddered in the twilight on the hill, seemingly anxiously waiting for the morning light to warm its weary walls. It felt so alone, so empty, despite being filled with tenants. How long had it been since it heard the banter of a precious child? How long had it been since it felt the coolness of fresh paint or contained the fragrance of unfettered laughter? As he knocked on the door, the man knew what waited inside, knew that there would be a coming calamity of sorts that would change the lives of those who hid from the world inside those walls.

The place had become aware of itself, of the history that echoed within the walls, a history not of compassion but of damnation and irrational superficiality. Yet, this man now standing there knew that he could somehow within make merriment mix with the pain and foster images of soft flowers with a scent of compassion. If the inside felt stagnant, just as a polluted river, it simply needed to actively flow again with the soft waters of human kindness.

He came to a door, faded green, paint curling with age, brass handle almost consumed by a thick network of scratches. And so on that day, with time unmeasured, someone came to the front door after the man softly knocked. The rotting wooden door creaked slowly open and echoing footsteps behind the person standing there invaded the silence that hung like a cloak around the house.

WHEN JESUS CAME TO LADYSMITH
TO BATTLE THE ANGEL OF DEATH

There, before him stood a portly woman of maybe fifty with a scowl on her face. Peeping over her shoulder, the stranger saw a thick worn carpet that clung to every object in the foyer as the rays of light shining through the old stained glass windows were catching on the particles of dust suspended in the stagnant air. The dust was floating about like soft snowflakes on a grey day in winter. There was a chill to the house that you just simply knew no amount of heat could ever totally obliterate.

The portly lady was abrupt. She curtly said, "Whatta you want?"

The man smiled understandingly, actually much more than understandingly. It was one of those rare smiles with a quality of eternal reassurance in it that you may come across four or five times in a lifetime. It seemed to face the cruel, unmerciful world for an instant, and then it concentrated on you with an irresistible prejudice in your favour. There was sincerity in both his smile and his voice. "I want to rent a room for awhile, with meals if possible."

Looking at him and rolling her eyes, she said, "You don't look like you can afford more than a blanket under an overpass."

"You would be surprised ma'am," he said as he reached into his pocket and pulled a roll of cash.

WHEN JESUS CAME TO LADYSMITH
TO BATTLE THE ANGEL OF DEATH

Her eyes lit up with delight and she said, "Well, do you want to rent by the week or by the month?"

"I'll start off weekly, please. I am not sure how long I will be here."

"Fine, breakfast is at 7:30, lunch is not included, but dinner is at 6:30. I am Diane Jenks. I see you have no luggage. Will it be arriving later?"

Again smiling with sincerity, the man said, "I will be buying what clothing I need. My name is Jesus."

Fighting back laughter, Mrs. Jenks said, "I guess you mean, 'Hay-soos don't you?"

With great preciseness, he replied, "No, I mean Jesus. I am not Spanish."

"Strange name."

"Not strange at all. I am sure you have heard it many times."

"I have, of course. Hope you will perform some miracles."

"Miracles, my dear woman, can be performed by many of us. The biggest miracle all us can perform is to stand against injustice."

J. Wayne Frye   45

WHEN JESUS CAME TO LADYSMITH
TO BATTLE THE ANGEL OF DEATH

Standing at the bottom of the stairs taking in the conversation between the two was Mary Jenks, Diane's daughter, who was intensely staring at Jesus. She, unlike her mother, was a young woman who sparkled with beauty. She had a kind of understated beauty, though. Perhaps it was because she was so disarmingly unaware of her prettiness. Her dark skin was completely flawless. She probably used no face creams or expensive beauty products to maintain a natural beauty which was hidden under plainness, a plainness that was, as Jesus assumed, forced on her by a draconian mother who was probably jealous of her good looks. She displayed absolute simplicity in its purest form, and from what Jesus would observe over time, a genuine fear of her mother.

"What are you staring at?" demanded Mrs. Jenks of her daughter.

"Wasn't staring," explained the meek Mary Jenks. "Was only thinking to myself about Jesus here. He is apparently used to people making fun of his name."

Smiling at her, Jesus said, "I am indeed, but a name is just a name. What is behind the name is what counts, and I hope I live up to what the name reflects, but what you read in the Bible is not the real story of Jesus. He was and is a rebel-rousing revolutionary who takes no prisoners, and accepts no excuses for cruelty and injustice."

WHEN JESUS CAME TO LADYSMITH
TO BATTLE THE ANGEL OF DEATH

Mary was an adult, but she was still a child inside when it came to fearing the world, fearing her mother. She was not overly tall and willowy, but more like an action star in a super hero movie. Yet, one could tell she was unaware of the beauty that was hidden in clothes that were about two sizes too big. Her muscle definition was perfect, but she walked with an excessively humble and frightened stride as she moved toward the two people at the front door. She was meek, not because of inherent meekness, but because she had, no doubt, been beaten down emotionally by a domineering mother, beat down to accept the fact that she was inferior and unworthy. Any psychologist would have probably deduced immediately that Diane Jenks was a woman, herself, with low self esteem, who covered up her own self-doubts by making her daughter feel useless and ignorant. She was genuinely jealous of her.

Mary moved steadily toward them and Jesus immediately noticed her perfect crimson hair that rested right above her shoulders and chocolate brown eyes that could swallow galaxies, but her shoulders were slightly hunched because she was carrying a heavy burden of immense emotional pain and there was no order in her terrible life. Everything, even the simplest things were already decided for her by a domineering, overbearing mother. She wanted and needed a change. She looked into Jesus' eyes, seeming to plead for release from her misery. She felt tears welling up in soft flickering eyes and smiled as she walked toward him. Her perfect skin was like silk over glass that looked fragile and soft, and the unerring amount of freckles around her nose all slow waltzed in a harmonious plea for help, for a hand up by a caring person, a hand up that would lift her from the misery she endured day in and day out.

Diane told her daughter to show Jesus around and take him to his room. Of course, first, she insisted on $250 in cash for the week's room and board, which Jesus cheerfully paid.

Mary was relatively quiet as she showed Jesus around, and the quietness solidified in his mind that she was a woman in the throes of pain acerbated by her meek nature that made her easy prey for a domineering mother.

As she showed him around his small, dingy room, she, with misty eyes, said, "I am glad you are here."

Her emotions were not easily hidden on her innocent face. Her pain was evident in the crease of her lovely brow and the down-curve of her full lips. But her eyes, her eyes showed her soul. They were a deep pool of restless misery, an ocean of hopeless grief. Pain turned her eyes into orbs of despondency, and in them he read clearly that she had long ago given up any hope of her life getting better. She had let the world break her.

Jesus, his eyes sparkling with sympathy, he said, "Do not allow anyone to force you to walk in darkness, because the darkness makes you stumble and fall both physically and emotionally. Those who walk in darkness want company in their misery. Do not allow them to force you to embrace their misery."

"It's hard," replied Mary.

"You know what is hard? It is hard to watch people accept their lot in life. The world is filled with people in misery, people who long for a modicum of justice, people who must struggle for sustenance while the few dine on caviar in their palaces of excess. Yet, the poor, the downtrodden, those on the margins of society far outnumber the greedy rich. There is power in numbers, but people are too complacent to rise up and demand justice. Those who try to arouse the marginalized are made out to be pariahs and systematically slaughtered by the powerful. Madero, Zapata, Luxemburg, Sandino, Trotsky, Gandhi, Evers, Malcolm X, King, Biko and the dearest of all revolutionaries – Che Guevara, all of them and so many more were eliminated, because they gave the forgotten hope. That is the way of a world where greed is promoted as an enviable trait. The world does not tolerate anyone who wants to lift up those who are forced to live in the darkness of economic and emotional misery. And my dear Mary, it is not just the rich who are enemies of hope. It is also those who bring emotional slavery to people. I can see your mental slavery. It is apparent that you allow yourself to be put upon, because you feel that you are not worthy of respect, not worthy of a good and decent life. You are worthy, more worthy than most. What is to be gained by accepting your own ball and chain that makes you an emotional cripple?"

Mary stood in awe of this man. Staring with tears in her eyes, she was amazed at his perceptible insights into her woes. She was so overwhelmed she could say nothing. All she did was just turn and sigh, and as she walked away, Jesus said, "Go in peace my child, go with the determination to change your life. The mountains, the hills and the valleys will break forth in joy before you, and all the trees will clap their hands in recognition of your right to be at peace with yourself."

It took no more than fifteen minutes for Mary to show Jesus around, but she felt as if she had been with him for hours so profound was the brief time she spent with him. She came back downstairs and her mother immediately asked, "So, what's he like?"

"Dunno," Mary replied.

WHEN JESUS CAME TO LADYSMITH
TO BATTLE THE ANGEL OF DEATH

"What's he like? Tell me. You have an opinion," demanded a sulking Diane.

"He is something special he is," replied Mary, with a glint in her eyes.

Almost laughing, Diane offered, "Of course he is. I mean he's the son of God, right?"

"He is the son of something he is, but I don't know what. He is like no man I ever seen in my entire life. He makes you feel like he knows what you are thinking."

"Poppycock," replied Diane as she ascended the stairs with a receipt for the rent to give him. She was shaking her head dismissingly as she was flabbergasted by her daughter's seeming lack of usual tepidness.

As she entered his room, Jesus was standing by the window looking out at the street below. He turned and bowed his head, saying nothing about her entering without knocking. Nothing could have been simpler than his courteous bow, yet there came with it a rush of knowledge indicating that he knew she was, like her daughter, in pain, but he did not show her the understanding glare he had shown Mary. Why? Because he saw through her façade of arrogance and she knew it, knew that he was a perceptive man capable of seeing deep within a person, capable of penetrating through the front so many of us put up. For one brief moment Diane saw her real self, the widow of a hard working janitor, a woman who had fallen into despair when her life of leisure suddenly fell apart because of a death, a death that made her into a disgruntled dowager with nothing but the property left her by a financially challenged husband, a property that she was still struggling to make payments on. It was but a momentary reflection though, caused by the intense glare of Jesus into her dark side. The next instant reality reasserted itself. Diane, existing precariously upon a daily round of petty meanness hurled at her daughter, extended her hand with the receipt and said. "Didn't know what last name to put."

Smiling, Jesus replied, "No need for a last name. I trust you ma'am, trust you implicitly to do the right thing, so I need no receipt. After all, what good is it to gain the whole world, but lose your soul? I am sure you are a woman of integrity, and I am just as sure your wonderful daughter is the light of your life, because she is so filled with grace and goodness that shines through her like the sun rising in the morning and burning away the darkness. You are indeed a lucky woman to have such a fine daughter."

Diane was in her own world, her own universe, and of any other than herself she could form no conception; she knew not length, nor breadth, nor height, for she had no experience of them; for she was herself the one and all, but deep inside she was a frightened little girl because her real being was absolutely nothing. There was no core to her dark soul.

She turned to leave but then turned back and said, "I wonder how you found me? I have not advertised the two empty rooms I have yet. Was going to do it tomorrow, actually, after they were cleaned and made presentable. Yours still needs cleaning, I will get it done. I promise."

"It is cleaned adequately. As for how I found you. Someone has recommended you," replied Jesus, as he treated the question as immaterial.

"Who? Who recommended my place?"

"You might not remember him," he smiled. "He thought that I should do well to pass the time I will be here in this lovely little town with you in this quiet place. You see, he said you were a kind and gentle woman, a woman of character."

Knowing he was lying, she replied, "Who? Who I want to know would say that of me?"

"Oh, he was a gentleman you may have forgotten, but he stayed here once long ago. He didn't give me his name, just said that I would find you an amenable person who would make me welcome, as you did him."

WHEN JESUS CAME TO LADYSMITH
TO BATTLE THE ANGEL OF DEATH

"How long ago was it when he stayed here? Surely he told you that?"

"Again, he gave me no real detail, just said what I have just shared with you."

Diane, puzzled, shot a quick glance at the stranger, but his face, though the gentle eyes were smiling, was frank and serious, as if he did not want to be challenged on who had suggested he stay there.

"At all events you will be comfortable here I hope. I can arrange to do your washing if you so desire. It will be an extra $7.50 a week." Then she pointed at the bathroom, as she said, "And please do not use an excess amount of water when showering, as the city keeps raising the rates."

Laughing, he replied, "Maybe I'll reduce my baths to once a week."

Smiling for some unknown reason, perhaps because he was a kind sort, Diane said, "Not if you plan to eat dinner at my table!"

Jesus had penetrated through Diane's starkness for a brief moment, as she felt a sense of kindness from him she received from few. And why should she sense any kindness from most people, when she was so incapable of showing any kindness herself?

WHEN JESUS CAME TO LADYSMITH
TO BATTLE THE ANGEL OF DEATH

Diane shot an obviously suspicious glance upon the stranger, and noticed that not a line was there upon that smooth fair face of his to which a sneer could for a moment have clung, but refused to show itself. Clearly, he was as simple as he looked. Or was he? There was a depth to this man she could not really fathom, a depth that seemed to indicate he understood things others did not, understood the machinations of personality that made people hide their real selves. She was, in a way, scared of this man, not scared of what he might do to her physically, but of what he might do to her emotionally.

He could see her consternation, as he said, "You have been very considerate to me, and I appreciate it. I feel Mrs. Jenks that I can leave myself entirely in your capable hands. Thank you for your hospitality."

She knew that he was being facetious when he complimented her on her hospitality, because deep inside she understood her own selfishness, her own total commitment to self at the expense of all others. She had an unbroken record for lacking civility, but at that moment, because of his manner, a manner that touched her deep within, she could not help but feel a tinge of kindness toward the stranger. That feeling made her angry with herself for allowing him to bring out within her that which she had long ago tossed away by embracing loathing self-pity.

WHEN JESUS CAME TO LADYSMITH
TO BATTLE THE ANGEL OF DEATH

She knew not what drove her, but she said to him, "I have made a mistake. I charged you $250 and it should have been $200. I'll give you the $50 back."

"I will not accept such sacrifice," exclaimed the stranger; "the $250 is fine and fair."

"No, $200 is what everyone else pays. Those are my terms," snapped Diane. "If you are bent on paying more, you can go elsewhere. You'll find plenty to oblige you. I will not be unfair to you."

Her vehemence for fairness impressed the stranger, but it did not impress Mrs. Jenks. In fact, she was appalled by her magnanimous nature and could not understand why she was acting as she was. What drove her to an unwillingness to take advantage of someone? It was not in her nature. She was shocked at herself.

"We will not contend further," he smiled. "I was merely afraid that in the goodness of your heart that you were being overly generous with an obvious man of meagre means."

"Oh, it isn't as good as all that," growled Mrs. Jenks.

"I am not so sure," returned the stranger. "I am impressed by you fairness. That is a rarity in today's world."

WHEN JESUS CAME TO LADYSMITH
TO BATTLE THE ANGEL OF DEATH

The stranger said, "Just keep the $50 and apply it to next week's rent as I am sure I will be here at least two weeks, probably longer."

Turning the doorknob, she looked back with soulful eyes and replied, "Of course, I can do that. I hope you get a good night's rest."

No one had ever had such an effect on Diane, and as she descended the stairs she kept reflecting back on the brief conversation and how he had obviously lied about her kindness. She was not kind and she knew it, and why she wondered had she been so foolish as to admit she had actually taken advantage of him by charging too much. She felt like a fool for letting his kind words manipulate her into admitting her chicanery and actually costing her $50.

Mary was standing in contemplation by the kitchen window, her hands leaning on the sink in front of her, when Diane entered the kitchen. By standing close to the window, one caught a glimpse of the trees in the small park across the street and through their almost bare branches of the darkening sky beyond.

Uncharacteristically nice, Diane said to her, "There's nothing much to do for the next half hour or so, till dinner time. I'll get dinner started for you, as you have worked very hard today. Maybe you'd like to go out for a stroll before dinner."

WHEN JESUS CAME TO LADYSMITH
TO BATTLE THE ANGEL OF DEATH

Shocked by her mother's nicety, she, with trembling voice replied, "That would be nice mother. Thank you so much. It's just the time of day I like best."

"Don't be longer than the half hour," shouted back Diane, surprised at her generosity of spirit toward her daughter.

Watching her daughter walk out the back door, Diane still could not get Jesus out of her mind. Why had she been so affected by him? Why did she let him manipulate her into being kind and honest? She took a deep breath and moved to the window, looking at the gathering clouds as twilight was fading into darkness. She knew that she was a woman as cold as ice, but for some reason, for a split second, in the presence of that man upstairs her cold heart had melted.

J. Wayne Frye

WHEN JESUS CAME TO LADYSMITH
TO BATTLE THE ANGEL OF DEATH

Chapter 3
His Heart Was Gone

Seek the source of the mystery.
Make an attempt to understand.
Plumb the depths of evil hearts
To sift through each grain of sand.

Aaron Adams was enjoying talking to the scholarly Porter, who had been, no doubt, deeply affected by the book about one of Aaron's most famous cases.

For a brief space no one moved until Stanley Chemer, with a sudden start of recollection, felt anxiously for his watch. He scanned its face eagerly, and then took a long, slow, deep breath.

WHEN JESUS CAME TO LADYSMITH
TO BATTLE THE ANGEL OF DEATH

He looked at Porter and said, with intensity, "The hour of reckoning is long past. Why not share with Mr. Adams why we have asked him here, and why the $10,000 check is a small price to pay for his expertise."

Porter, his eyes twinkling, said, "Mr. Adams, we have a mystery that even Arthur Conan Doyle's Sherlock Holmes would, no doubt, find beyond his abilities to solve, so we elected to hire the modern equivalent, the detective celebrated in best selling books by our local novelist, Wayne Frye."

At these unexpected words, which carried in them something of the tone of a challenge, the undaunted Aaron eased back into his chair and said, "Go ahead then. Challenge me."

Porter continued, "It is a mystery that has baffled the minds of the local RCMP (Royal Canadian Mounted Police) detectives."

"I have heard nothing of it. Tell me more," replied Aaron.

Porter, flushed uncomfortably and picked uneasily at the arm of his chair. "No one but the police have heard of it," he murmured, "and they only through those of us here in this room. It is a remarkable crime, to which, unfortunately, we are the only people who know about it for now." He took a deep breath and looked over at a man who had been introduced as Calvin Hobbs, as if to indicate he should continue the discussion.

"I am," offered Hobbs, inclining his head politely, "the USA charge-de-affairs in Victoria. Had I not been detained by the police I would have started this morning back to my post in the capitol city, Victoria."

"Do you hear, Mr. Adams?" cried Charles Porter jubilantly with almost a laugh. "Can anyone imagine an American diplomat being questioned by the Canadian police? What an outrage to expect an American to be held for questioning. We all know important Americans are above the law, above any law, especially in America, where those of importance never have to pay the piper!"

Another gentleman, who had been the quietest member there, Clarence Manly, interrupted with so pronounced an exclamation of excitement and delight that Porter ceased speaking. "I, Mr. Adams, must say that Mr. Porter, not I or anyone else here, was the one who wanted to lure you to try and analyze the mystery for us."

Aaron, scanning the faces of the gentleman there, said with a note of true sincerity, "I am certainly not immune to seeking out financial rewards for my work, and I must admit that I found the $10,000 retainer tempting. Please go on, and I may yet accept the retainer."

WHEN JESUS CAME TO LADYSMITH
TO BATTLE THE ANGEL OF DEATH

With an extremely annoyed look toward Clarence Manly, Hobbs said, "I, of course, have diplomatic immunity, but I have agreed to stay in Canada for awhile to get this matter sorted out, which is why we have decided, at the behest of Mr. Porter, to contact you, Mr. Adams. This is a most extraordinarily baffling case, which requires the most astute of detecting skills, a person with an extraordinary acumen for deductive reasoning."

Hobbs turned to Manly and said, "Please relate why he is here, Clarence."

"Mr. Adams," said Manly, "as an American diplomat, it is extraordinary that Mr. Hobbs was halted by our police, but he indeed was because he is the only witness of a most remarkable crime; in fact, one of the most remarkable crimes I believe that has ever been committed in the province of British Columbia., assuming it was committed.

Hobbs moved his head in assent and glanced at the others there. They were looking doubtfully at him, and the face of each showed that they were all greatly perplexed as Hobbs said, "The crime is exceptional indeed to justify the police interfering with a representative of a friendly power."

Another gentleman, Dr. Harley Borden, leaned toward Aaron, and motioned toward the $10,000 check. "That will be a small price to pay if you can solve this mystery."

WHEN JESUS CAME TO LADYSMITH
TO BATTLE THE ANGEL OF DEATH

Chemer interjected with sincerity, "Mr. Porter, just tell him about this remarkable crime."

Porter nodded vigorously. After first glancing toward the door, as if concerned that it was definitely closed, he leaned forward across the coffee table. The others drew their chairs nearer and bent toward him.

"Of course," said Porter, "I hope you understand that I am speaking in confidentiality. The confidences of this club are inviolate. Until the police give the facts to the public press, I must consider all here my confederates. You have heard nothing; you know no one connected with this mystery. Even I must remain anonymous in regards to this outside this room."

The gentlemen seated around him nodded gravely, a couple murmuring, "of course."

Aaron reached down and took the $10,000 check, placing it inside his coat breast pocket, as he said, "A retainer means I have a moral obligation to keep my clients' confidentiality. I will return all but a dollar of this if I do not accept the case. That way, your $1 retainer means I am bound to confidentiality.

"We will refer to this case henceforth," said Charles Porter, "as the case of the reluctant attaché."

WHEN JESUS CAME TO LADYSMITH
TO BATTLE THE ANGEL OF DEATH

Porter then turned to Hobbs and said, "It is more your story than mine. Please lay out the details."

Hobbs looked almost reluctant, but began his story. "Two days ago I arrived in Ladysmith for a brief respite before returning on business to Washington, D.C., and because there is only one hotel here, I booked a room there. I know very few people in Ladysmith, except for Mr. Porter and the gentlemen here, all of whom encouraged me to become a temporary guest member of the club some time ago. Now, in Washington I had become pals with an officer in the Canadian navy who retired, and who was temporarily living in a boarding house just up the street from here, while awaiting the construction of a home overlooking the Georgia Strait, a home that is slowly taking form, but because of its high location and no road access is projected to take up to one year to build. I had received a most hearty invitation to visit with him. He left me the number of the boarding house where he lived, but for some reason forgot to give me his cell phone number. I called the boarding house, and a most disagreeable woman answered the phone and flatly refused to call him to the phone, as she said he was upstairs in his room, and she had no inclination to climb the stairs as she was busy. Anyway, she stated that she did not run an answering service for her guests, so I should call him on his cell. When I said I didn't have that number, she replied that was my problem not hers and hung up on me."

WHEN JESUS CAME TO LADYSMITH
TO BATTLE THE ANGEL OF DEATH

"So, I got the address of the boarding house, which is in a converted church, and I walked up to see my old acquaintance. It is quiet a climb up the hill to where it is located, so I was pretty exhausted when I knocked on the door. I was greeted by a young woman of a very agreeable nature, who was the daughter of the woman, whom I assumed, had slammed the phone down on me. It was surprising to find someone of such a kind disposition was related to such an obvious ogre. She very graciously showed me to my friend's room. He suggested we eat out, as the guests there were, according to his astute observation, mostly very uncongenial and the food served was mediocre at best. We dined at a place called *Jack's* and talked over our old days in Washington and Haiti when I was at the State Department and he was a Naval Attaché. We lamented the current state of affairs in the USA, which both of us felt had descended to a near dictatorship and Third World status under the current buffoon inhabiting the White House. After discussing the abominable nature of the current American political scene and laughing over some of our past adventures, we strolled back up that infernal hill to the boarding house, where we sat in his room for awhile and continued talking. I told him, about nine o'clock, that I must get back to the hotel, so he took out his cell phone and called for a cab. I should have asked for his cell number at the time, but much to my regret, maybe because I was so tired, I did not."

WHEN JESUS CAME TO LADYSMITH
TO BATTLE THE ANGEL OF DEATH

"For the next quarter of an hour, as we sat talking while waiting for the cab, we were surprised no taxi arrived. He called again, and the dispatcher said that there was a rash of cab requests, and it would be at least an hour before she could get a cab there. I signalled to my friend to cancel, because I was only about two kilometres away and could just walk."

You could sense that there was much consternation in Hobbs's recounting of the tale, as he continued. "So, he got up and walked over to his window, looking out into the darkness. He called to me, pointing out the intense fog that was gathering. He asked if I was sure I wanted to walk in the fog that was so dense one could barely see a hand in front of your face. He even commented that he had never in his life seen such a dense fog. I joined him at the window, but I could see nothing, as it was so dark. Had I not known that the house looked out upon the street I would have believed that I was facing a dark wall. I raised the sash and stretched out my hand, but still I could see nothing. Even the light of the streetlamps opposite and the lights in the windows of the houses across the street had been smothered in the densely greying mist. The lights of the room in which I stood penetrated the fog only to the distance of a few centremetres from my eyes. A vast blanket of thick mist hung heavy over everything. It suffocated every building, every home and every tree, swallowing every distant

J. Wayne Frye

object and vanishing around every corner. It crept all around the boarding house like the darkness of the day of the crucifixion. Its silent footsteps were tiptoeing around the sidewalk, even hiding it from view. It was as if I was lulled to sleep by it."

Hobbs appeared to be in a trance-like state as he became almost psychologically lost in what was obviously a frightening experience for him. "How can I adequately describe a fog that was like a giant eraser moving indiscriminately to eradicate what was once there into something that was not there anymore. It made you feel as if you went into it that you would be swallowed, erased, eradicated by this enveloping greyness. It hurt the eyes it was so grey. Staring at it made me feel like I was staring into a deep, dark abyss where something evil waited. It was almost hypnotic."

"I must admit that I was frightened by that fog, but I told my friend I needed to go. So I did go. Yes, I went with great trepidation into that infernal fog. My friend went with me to the front door, and asked me if I wanted him to walk with me, but I said a very definite no to his request. I had walked there twice counting my trip to *Jack's* with my friend, and assumed I could feel my way along the row of houses set back only slightly from the sidewalk. That would bring me to the cross street, which was First Avenue, where I would turn left, walk down First Avenue for two blocks past *Jack's* again, and then all I had to do was make a right onto High Street and my hotel was only about 500 metres from there. A piece of cake I thought."

"The greying fog wrapped around me like a blanket, the familiar sights from my previous walk up the hill laid mysterious, hiding and looming out at me in a greyed haze like images from a horror movie that had frightened me in my youth. I held out my hand in front of me and watched it become partially obscured. My mind began to dance with images of someone in the dark chanting spells, conjuring the mist like a deranged witch drunk on her own powers, cackling, eyes twinkling with evil. I could not see anything in that fog, but my mind was beginning to convince me that I was not alone. Someone was following me."

"As my heart pounded, I turned tepidly onto First Avenue, and there were no others out, and there were no cars on the street. The silence in that greyness was almost deafening, as I passed a row of shops until I got to High Street and turned right."

"I heard a noise from a considerable distance behind me, and I turned in the direction from which I had just come, and I saw a square of faint light cut into the grey fog. Silence fell upon me then, and I was left alone in a dripping darkness. I have never known such a fog as that night, and it was not just the fog. There was something else, something indiscernible, a feeling. It was a fog which was now springing from the paved streets and crawling upon everything in sight, even crawling upon me, as I very meekly moved slowly forward. There was a house to my right that I could barely make out. It was more an outline than anything else. There was a white fence around the house, and I placed my hand on it to maintain my balance. I took my hand off after awhile and moved forward, but again started to lose my balance, so I reached out for the fence, but it was gone, completely disappeared and the further I moved to find it the further I seemed to be sinking into space. I had the unpleasant conviction that at any moment I might step over a precipice. Since I had set out I had encountered no one, but now I could distinguish the occasional footfalls of pedestrians, but they were heard not seen. Several times I called aloud, and once a jocular gentleman answered me, but only to ask me where I thought he was, and then even he was swallowed up in the silence. Just above me I could make out a faint light across the street, which I guessed came from a streetlamp, and I moved across the street, dearly hoping no car would be coming, for if it was there was no way I could be seen. Other than the flicker of light, which was no larger than the tip of my finger, I could distinguish nothing about me. I did hear muffled voices, but I could not tell from whence they came, and I heard the scrape of a foot moving cautiously. Then I heard a muffled cry as someone apparently stumbled behind me."

J. Wayne Frye 69

WHEN JESUS CAME TO LADYSMITH
TO BATTLE THE ANGEL OF DEATH

"So dense was the fog that I was afraid to move. I decided that until someone took me in tow I had best remain where I was, and it must have been for five minutes that I waited by a streetlamp, straining my ears to hear anything in the greyness of the night. In a house near me some people were listening to what sounded like a funeral dirge on a blaring radio. I even fancied I could hear the windows shake to the rhythm of their feet, but I could not make out more than the general outline of the house. Sometimes, as the music rose, it seemed close at my hand, and again, to be floating high in the air above my head. Although I was surrounded by houses on the street I felt as alone as a man on a deserted island."

Aaron was growing weary of his vividly exaggerated descriptions, but elected not to ask him to speed up his rendition of the tale out of fear he might leave something highly germane out. Years of detecting had made him astutely aware that a small detail might be the clue that leads to solving a case.

Hobbs continued. "There seemed to be no reason to expect the fog to lift, so I decided to edge my way down the street toward my hotel which was on the Trans Canada Highway at the end of the street. I again set out, and at once bumped against a low iron fence. At first I believed this to be an area railing, but on following it I found that it stretched for a long distance, and that it was pierced at an interval with a gate. I was standing uncertainly with my hand on the gate when a square of light suddenly opened in the night, and in it I saw an immaculately dressed young gentleman, and back of him were the lights of a hall. I guessed from its elevation and distance from the sidewalk that this light must come from the door of a house set back from the street, and I determined to approach it and ask this man to tell me where I was. But in fumbling with the lock of the gate I instinctively bent my head, and when I raised it again the door had partly closed, leaving only a narrow shaft of light. Whether the man had re-entered the house, or had left it I could not tell, but I hastened to open the gate, and as I stepped forward I found myself upon a concrete walkway. At the same instant there was the sound of quick steps upon the walkway, and someone rushed past me. I called to him, but he made no reply, and I heard the gate click and the footsteps hurrying away upon the sidewalk."

"Under ordinary circumstances, the person's rudeness and his recklessness in dashing so hurriedly through the mist would have struck me as peculiar, but everything was so distorted by the fog that at the moment I did not consider it. The door was still as he had left it, partly opened. I went up the path and after much fumbling found the door-bell button and gave it a sharp pounding. The bell answered me from a great depth and distance, but no movement followed from inside the house, and although I pushed the bell again I could hear nothing. Also, the music had ceased when the man ran out of the house."

"I was anxious to be on my way, but unless I knew where I was going there was little chance of my making any speed, and I was determined that until I learned my bearings I would not venture back into the infernal fog. So, why I do not know, but throwing caution to the wind, I pushed the door all the way open and stepped inside the house. I found myself in a long and narrow hallway, upon which doors opened from either side. At the end of the hall was a staircase with a sweeping curve. The banister was covered with heavy Persian rugs, and the walls of the hall were also hung with them. The door on my left was closed, but the one nearer me on the right was open, and as I stepped opposite to it I saw that it was a sort of reception or waiting-room, and that it was empty. The door below it was also open, and with the idea that I would surely find someone there, I walked on up the hall. I was wearing a suit and tie, so I felt that I did not look like a burglar; consequently, I had no great fear of being gunned down, as this was Canada; not America, where guns are as prevalent as flies. The second door in the hallway opened into a dining room. This was also empty. However, it appeared not to be used as a dining room at all, because there were no chairs around the table. The greater part of the room was empty."

WHEN JESUS CAME TO LADYSMITH
TO BATTLE THE ANGEL OF DEATH

Aaron liked a good tale as much as anyone, but he was beginning to get antsy, waiting for the story to come to a conclusion, but it appeared that Hobbs was not going to be rushed. In fact, he seemed to enjoy building suspense.

Noticing Aaron's obvious impatience Hobbs said, "I am getting there Mr. Adams. Just be patient, please. So, by this time I had grown conscious of the fact that I was wandering about in a strange house, and that, apparently, I was alone in it. The silence of the place began to try my nerves, and in a sudden, unexplainable panic I started for the open entry door. But as I turned, I saw a man sitting on a bench at the curve of the stairs in the hallway, which had been hidden from me. His eyes were shut, and he was sleeping soundly. The very moment before I had been bewildered, because I could see no one, but at the sight of this man I was much more bewildered. He was a very thin man, moderately tall if he had stood, with long curly hair which hung around his shoulders. He was dressed in a black shirt that went to over his waist and hung outside his pants. I advanced and touched the man on the shoulder, and after an effort he awoke, and, on seeing me, sprang to his feet and began bowing rapidly and making deprecatory gestures. He profusely apologized for having fallen asleep, and I was able to explain to him that I desired some directions. He seemed unable to understand what I was saying, perhaps, I assumed, because he was still

J. Wayne Frye   73

waking up. He nodded vigorously, and very deliberately said, 'the angel will address your concerns' as he walked toward the end of the hall with me tepidly following."

"I distinctly made out the word 'angel,' and I was near raucous laughter. I had thought it would be easy enough to explain my intrusion to an average man, but explaining it to an angel was another matter, and as I followed him down the hallway I was somewhat puzzled by the dark nature of the place and wondered where all the noise of partying people and the music had come from just a minute or so before. As we advanced, he noticed that the front door was standing open, and with an exclamation of surprise, hastened quickly back toward it and closed it. Then he rapped twice on the door of what was apparently the den. There was no reply to his knock, and he tapped again, and then timidly, and cringing subserviently, opened the door and stepped inside. He withdrew himself at once and stared stupidly at me, shaking his head."

"He turned with a startled look on his face and said, 'he is not there.' He stood for a moment gazing blankly through the open door, and then hastened toward the dining room and stood staring at an empty room. He came back and pointed upward and said, 'he is above. I will inform the angel of your presence.' Then he walked up the stairs."

WHEN JESUS CAME TO LADYSMITH
TO BATTLE THE ANGEL OF DEATH

"The man had left me standing in the dark hallway, so I stepped into the den and took a seat to wait, because I thought it would be rude to just dart out back into the fog. Anyway, I wanted to see this person he was calling an angel. Not taking a seat, I noticed a large Persian rug on the floor and it looked like it had just been hurriedly placed down on the floor as it was slightly askew in terms of symmetry. Near the front bay window was a grand piano, and at the other end of the room a carved figure of an evil looking clown. Then, there was a huge dark screen with a canopy of silken draperies above it that formed a sort of alcove. In front of the alcove was spread the skin of a black bear, and set on that was a small coffee table. It held a lighted incense candle and two solid gold candelabras. I had heard no movement from above, and it must have been several minutes that I stood waiting, noting these details of the room and wondering at the delay, and at the strange silence that permeated the entire place. And then suddenly I saw projecting from behind the screen as though it were stretched along the back of a sofa, the hand of a man and the lower part of his arm. I was as startled as though I had come across a footprint on a deserted island. Evidently the man had been sitting there ever since I had come into the room, probably even ever since I had entered the mysterious house, and he had heard the servant knocking upon the door, and he had obviously heard the servant come into the room but ignored him. I was dumbfounded."

J. Wayne Frye 75

WHEN JESUS CAME TO LADYSMITH
TO BATTLE THE ANGEL OF DEATH

"I thought over why he had not acknowledged the servant or me, and assumed he was simply a rude person. I could see nothing of him except his hand, part of his arm and the back of his head, but I had an unpleasant feeling that he had been peering at me through the reflection in the window to his right. I moved slowly toward him and said, 'I beg your pardon.' As I stood there near the back of the sofa, looking at my own reflection in the window and at the back of his head waiting for a reply, I got absolutely no acknowledgement whatsoever. Furthermore, the hand and the arm did not stir. Apparently the man was hell-bent upon ignoring me, but all I wished was to apologize for my intrusion and to leave the strange house. Yet, I was motivated, as if by some unknown force, to walk into the alcove and peer at the person. Inside the alcove was a sofa piled with cushions, and on the end of it nearer me the man was sitting. He was a middle-aged man with light blond hair and, despite wearing a dark blue suit, indicated he had a rather obvious Herculean-like physique. His attitude was one of complete ease and apparent disinterest in me. However, I mistook that disinterest at being directed at me, because on his face was burned an expression of utter horror. I realized his disinterest was no intended slight toward me. You see, the man was obviously dead."

At this point, Aaron's interest was piqued, and he said, "Finally, we have reached the high point."

WHEN JESUS CAME TO LADYSMITH
TO BATTLE THE ANGEL OF DEATH

Hobbs took a deep breath and said, "Yes, and that is why I wanted to take my time and set the scene, because I think it important to show just how shocking it was to me. For a flash of time I was too startled to act, but in the same flash I was convinced that the man had met his death from no accident, and that he had not died through any ordinary method like a heart attack or stroke. The expression on his face was much too terrible to be misinterpreted as anything other than a surprise ending to his life. The look on his face spoke as eloquently as any words could have. It told me that before the end came he had seen, experienced, actually fell victim to unmitigated horror of the foulest kind. I was so sure he had been murdered that I instinctively looked on the floor for a weapon, and, at the same moment, out of concern for my own safety, quickly turned to look behind me, but the silence of the house continued unbroken."

"Now, I do not want to be overly dramatic, but without comprehending the fear caused by that evil place and that horrible silence one cannot be fully aware of the horror of the situation in which I found myself. Whatever can silence be? For is there not always the sound of your own heart? Blackness is a canvass for nightmares, and the room, at that moment in time, seemed to be bathed in blackness. And so as the quietness grew deeper I could hear my own steady rhythm from within, the rhythm of my own growing horror in a place I surmised pulsated with evil. I felt a shaking of my limbs as I tried to suppress the shock of what I was observing. And all the while I was drinking in the silence that elevated the fear engulfing me. The silence was only slightly altered by the intensity of my own breathing. My blood was cold as arctic air that hangs limp in the darkness, bringing shivers and making teeth feel as if the mouth is opened they will crack from the glaciation of everything that breathes. The silence was becoming a poison to me, for in that void of sound, as I looked at that dead body, the shallowness of life struck home just like the recycled, re-hashed, twitterized garbage worthy of Fox News. How does one properly describe the scariness of the silence in that room, that room with only me and the dead body? Or was there something else there, something else waiting to do to me what had been done to that thing on the sofa? Silence gnawed at my insides. No, it gnawed at my soul, gnawed deep within me, sent a chill that froze me in place. That infernal silence hung in the air like the suspended moment before a falling glass shatters on the floor. The silence was like a gaping void, needing to be filled with sounds, words, anything, but there was nothing, nothing at all. The silence clung to me like a poisonous cloud that at any moment could choke the life from me and put me in the same state as that thing on the sofa. The silence seeped into my every pore, like a poison slowly paralyzing me, making me devoid of any speech or movement."

WHEN JESUS CAME TO LADYSMITH
TO BATTLE THE ANGEL OF DEATH

"I, for some reason, recalled as I stared down at the man's glassy eyes, the movie *Apocalypse Now*. I kept intensely thinking about what that great actor, Marlon Brando, who played Colonel Walter E. Kurtz, kept saying as he lay dying on the cave floor, slaughtered with a machete brandished by Captain Willard, "The horror, the horror, the horror."

"I have seen a great number of dead men in my 68 years, particularly because I was in that illegal, immoral abomination called the Vietnam War, a war that also had immense horrors, but that was a mass horror, and I shared that wretched horror with others, but this horror I was facing was not shared. I was all alone trapped in that damnable silence. So a dead man, for the single reason that he is dead, did not repel me, and, though I knew that there was no hope that this man was alive, still for some reason I felt compelled to feel his pulse."

"As I did so, I kept my ears alert for any sound from the floors above me. The man on the sofa was in formal dress, with his suit jacket neatly buttoned. I unbuttoned the jacket and got a tinge of some liquid on my fingers. I stood there in horror as I pulled back the jacket. There, in the wide bosom of his shirt I found a gaping slit in the garment and skin that had obviously been opened with a long sharp blade, but what was more despicable than the torn flesh opened up with a curved blade, no doubt, was what was not there. Horror of horrors, his heart was gone."

WHEN JESUS CAME TO LADYSMITH
TO BATTLE THE ANGEL OF DEATH

Chapter 4
Twinkling That Signified Fear

There is a man of quiet peace
Who walks among the afflicted
In a world that flounders in darkness,
But do not mistake his calm demeanour
For acquiescence to the villainy
That permeates societies
Based on demented greed and evil,
For within him beats the heart
Of a revolutionary who would
Make Che Guevara seem meek.

The man named Jesus did not show up for dinner, but those assembled after dinner in the drawing-room discussed the stranger with that freedom and frankness characteristic of gossipers towards the absent.

Aubrey Long, who fancied himself a bit of a bon vivont, said, "What I call a man of mystery, because he arrives with no bag wearing worn-out clothing which indicates a man of little means and stays in his room rather than come down for dinner. Not very smart Mrs. Jenks if you ask me, assuming he has paid for both room and board."

"He has paid, yes," responded Mrs. Jenks.

"Speaking for myself," commented Ileana Rabe, "haven't seen him, but heard him singing in his room, singing some AC/DC song from long ago about evil. Sounds like a preacher man maybe to me."

Black shadow hangin' over your shoulder
Black mark up against your name
Your green eyes couldn't get any colder
There's bad poison runnin' through your veins

Evil walks behind you
Evil sleeps beside you
Evil talks arouse you
Evil walks behind you

Black widow weavin' evil notions
Dark secrets bein' spun in your web
Good men goin' down in your ocean

WHEN JESUS CAME TO LADYSMITH
TO BATTLE THE ANGEL OF DEATH

They can't swim 'cause they're tied to your bed

Evil walks behind you
Evil sleeps beside you
Evil talks arouse you
Evil walks behind you

You just cry wolf
I sometimes wonder
Where you park your broom
Oh black widow

C'mon weave your web
Down in your ocean
You got 'um tied to your bed
With your dark, dark secrets
And your green, green eyes
You black widow

Evil walks behind you
Evil sleeps beside you
Evil talks arouse you
Evil walks behind you
Evil walks so bad
In a world so sad

Songwriters: B. Johnson / A. Young / M. Young
Evil Walks lyrics © BMG Rights Management

Aubrey offered an observation based on nothing but his innate prejudice. "He ain't no white man for sure. You can see he is a mixed breed. He is. Yeah, those are the kind who straddle two worlds and aren't welcome in either world. They are just the mongrels of the human race."

"I was walking by his door when he was singing," said the mousey Marie Kemp. "I just stayed by the door for awhile and listened. Suddenly, he opened the door and just stood there smiling at me, but kept singing, finishing the song. Well, it made me feel good just looking at him. There was something calming about his demeanour. There was something almost magical in the way he introduced himself to me. His name should have elicited a laugh from me, but I could not laugh at him. No, I felt if I laughed it would be a personal affront to him, and the way he spoke so calm and so reverent made me respectful, but also fearful, so fearful of offending him. Then it was his clothes, I suppose, clothes a bit ragged and torn, and a bit oversized that made me pity him, pity him for probably not being able to afford better. Then I realized that he was the kind of person if he had millions of dollars would still shop at the thrift store, because he put no credence in show like I am afraid I do. I spend too much on clothes to cover up my lack of sophistication I suppose, but for him, I believe he knows it is not the clothes that make the man, but the real man within that makes the man. He can say more with his eyes, those hazel eyes that are intensely observant, so observant that they seem to be dancing with kindness, but at the same time saying with their intense clarity of purpose that it would not be advisable to get on his wrong side, to question his sincerity, to dare challenge his righteousness of purpose."

"Yes, it would be his clothes that would make you think he is of meagre means. I believe he, based upon brief words with him in the hallway, is also of meagre intellect," drawled the languid Virginia Davis, a tall, shapely woman with an air of haughtiness, engaged at that moment in futile efforts to recline with elegance and comfort combined upon an obviously uncomfortable sofa. Her legs with muscular thighs crossed seductively, which were attracting the attention she craved from all men, was just her way of proving to herself that her worth was more in her looks than anything else. Inside, she was wondering why, when she met Jesus in the hallway, he had not shown the usual prurient interest exhibited by most men. It bothered her when a man seemed to not be titillated as a result of her alluring nature. "Yeah," she thought, "he must be gay."

Ms. Marie Kemp, having secured the only easy-chair in the room, resented the attention Virginia was getting from the men. Then again, she always did resent the fact that her clothes, which she could not really afford, seemed an inadequate way to get the attention from men she so desperately desired. Without hesitation, she said to Virginia, "Is that intended to be clever or only rude? Apparently you did not see the same man I did."

WHEN JESUS CAME TO LADYSMITH
TO BATTLE THE ANGEL OF DEATH

"I intended it to be both rude and clever." claimed Virginia.

"Myself, I must confess," shouted the older and self-considered wiser, Cap Johnson, "I found him a fool during our brief conversation."

"I noticed you seemed to be getting on very well together," purred his wife, a plump little lady with a tinge of arrogance in her manner.

"Possibly we were," retorted Johnson. "Fate has accustomed me to a society of fools. The world is afflicted with fools I am afraid. That is why people don't always vote for the Conservative party. The fools vote for liberal minded people so the government can give away things free to those who are a drain on society. He struck me as an interesting fellow, but one who does not understand the world as it is, but is rather a do-gooder who believes the poor deserve a hand-up, which only makes them more dependent, in my opinion. He may have the name Jesus, but he needs to follow the advice of the apostle Paul who said, 'He who does not work, neither shall he eat.' Just my opinion for what it's worth."

The usually meek Mary Jenks, to the surprise of all there, offered an astute observation. "It seems to me Jesus, in the Bible I read, does not conjure up a vengeful, spiteful, jealous God, but a God of love who extends the hand of compassion. I see in that man now here among us a kind, caring, non-judgmental human being who has a great capacity for reaching out, but I also see in him a revolutionary spirit that desires to light a fire in a forest of economic and emotional suffering that will destroy greed and the pure evil of selfishness that is, in today's capitalistic society, making slaves of the 99% in service to the 1% who can never get enough." She then rose and walked to the kitchen, as all there sat in awe of the lucid observation from the usually quiet and demure young woman.

"Well, he has, without a doubt, certainly had a profound effect on your sweet daughter," said Cap Johnson to the obviously equally shocked Mrs. Jenks.

Surprised at her daughter's sudden found ability to speak her mind, Mrs. Jenks said, "Yes, I have noticed that myself, despite the fact he didn't strike me as much of a conversationalist. I was not aware you had all met him."

They all looked at one another, as Jesus walked into the room. No, perhaps sauntered would be a better word, as he headed for the one vacant chair and said, "Good evening all; I am sorry I was late for dinner," and as he made a quick sweeping motion over his clothes, he continued, "I found that the thrift store was open late and bought some new old clothes."

WHEN JESUS CAME TO LADYSMITH
TO BATTLE THE ANGEL OF DEATH

What clothing says about a person is often a misnomer. A person may dress for success, and it might be sage advice not to go to a job interview in torn or ragged clothing, but there are some people who have a commanding presence no matter what they wear. Obviously, the clothes Jesus was wearing had been worn many times before, until discarded by someone who thought they were too old to display the proper impression any longer. Yet, on Jesus they were not just old clothes from a thrift store. They were an idyllic example of how he viewed life, viewed his own lack of concern with what others might think of him. Still, even in old and somewhat ragged clothes, he was an imposing presence.

Some folks wear a smile, Jesus was the smile. Everything about him was soft and understated knowledge, as he greeted each person with a knowing nod. His voice had a softness that put people at ease with the way he simply said "hello" and every step he took was as if in slow motion compared to almost anyone else. He bent forward slightly but his head was always held high as he appeared to glide rather than walk. The pace of his footsteps did not change as every motion seemed a way of him indicating he was a man to be respected. Still, one could see he carried heavy burdens, but refused to allow them to control him, as it was evident that when your world explodes from the inside he was the kind of man you wanted next to you. He could feel the shockwave of trouble and stay on his feet. Whatever had to be done he was the man who could get it done or die trying. By his bearing, you knew he could cover every angle and stay right there until you could breathe, walk and talk with determination. Once the storm passed, his tolerance for backward steps would be all but non-existent. His shoulder was only for crying on when you couldn't stand alone. After that he expected you to build inner strength, resilience, and to not expect flowers on birthdays, gifts at Christmas or impulsive purchases, because commercialism left him cold and indifferent. His relationship currency was a hug, careful words and thoughtful deeds that you could lock in the vault of hope.

As Jesus eased into a chair, Aubrey asked "Know anything significant?"

"The most significant thing I know is that we live in a world where mankind has accepted his own despicable condition, has bowed before the commercialization of everything and refused to stand against the tyranny of the privileged class that enslaves him. Lining up for your own ball and chains is a result of despair; the despair that nothing will ever get better, that life is not to be lived, but to simply be an eternal struggle to keep your head above raging waters that engulf you."

"Seems a bit of a morose outlook," stated Virginia Davis.

WHEN JESUS CAME TO LADYSMITH
TO BATTLE THE ANGEL OF DEATH

"Oh, it is a morose outlook, because the truth is the world is an extremely morose place. People are brainwashed into believing that happiness is a BMW and a Mercedes in a two car garage, a $150,000 RV in the backyard of a house that comes with a payment that requires constant struggle to make every month. People are in a vicious cycle of acquiring things, but never acquiring satisfaction. People cruise by the homeless in doorways, in vacant lots or standing in food lines, not giving any thought to the plight of those individuals cast aside by an economic system that rewards greed. The government blames laziness rather than a system setup to reward those at the top. Opulent churches are built to the glory of God, while God prefers feeding the poor to feeding the egos and pocketbooks of those who preach his word. While a pompadoured, $3000 suit wearing prancing buffoon pontificates in the pulpit, God, if there is one, hangs his head in disgusting shame at the pompous finger-pointing hypocrisy of those who sit in luxurious pews absorbing the presumptuous propaganda spewed out by those who have no idea what real religion is."

"I beg your pardon," said Aubrey.

"It is I who should beg yours," replied a reticent Jesus in his soft low voice, "I beg your pardon for being so passionate about what the world should be rather than what it is, but that is who I am."

WHEN JESUS CAME TO LADYSMITH
TO BATTLE THE ANGEL OF DEATH

"Are you staying long in Ladysmith?" asked Ileana, raising her eyes towards the stranger.

"Not long," answered Jesus. "At least I hope it is not long, although I must say this is a magnificently beautiful place, which, if I had the time, I would enjoy a lengthy sojourn here."

"Tell me about yourself. You interest me," offered Virginia Davis, adopting an authoritative air towards Jesus.

"Well, I am glad I interest you, but I am afraid that I am a pretty ordinary person who should be of little interest to a beautiful sophisticated lady like you." The way he said it made her actually feel ugly without him using the word. He continued, "I am but a poor wayfarer on the road of life with little to offer but observational analysis of the plight experienced by the least among us. And that tendency often erects a barrier between me and others."

"You're a very bold person with your rhetoric," Virginia said as Ileana Rabe lowered her head, but not her eyes that were encountering the eyes of the stranger named Jesus looking deeply into hers. And then it was that Ileana experienced a curious sensation when Jesus gave her a slow, methodical smile spreading over his face as his eyes twinkled with an all-knowing gaze that indicated with this man something very bad could happen or very

WHEN JESUS CAME TO LADYSMITH
TO BATTLE THE ANGEL OF DEATH

good, depending on the person's perspective. It seemed to Ileana that she was no longer the woman who had walked into the room and looked into the mirror over the marble mantelpiece with mild disgust for herself, for now she felt as if she was a cheerful, bright-eyed lady verging on middle age, yet still good-looking in spite of her faded complexion and somewhat thin brown locks. She looked over at the obviously beautiful Virginia Davis and felt no usual pang of jealousy shoot through her, as she, because of that knowing smile from Jesus, seemed, on the whole, a more attractive lady than Virginia. She suddenly realized that beauty was more than mere looks. It was about attitude, and that smile and those twinkling eyes from Jesus had infused deep within her a new attitude. There was a wholesome feeling that permeated through her body simply because of that smile that elevated her self esteem without any words being spoken by Jesus.

Turning his gaze from Ileana, Jesus looked over at Virginia. Another grin lit up his face now as instead of bringing relief to Virginia, his gaze made her wish she could bolt from the room, because she knew instinctively that he could see through her facade of arrogant self-satisfaction based on her physical beauty. He was able to comprehend the depths of her self-doubt, because he understood that the moon for most of each month is dark in part, and that uncertainty danced in the night while many of us harboured within a terror of vacillation that rages in the murkiness of our souls, for upon the light of hope hath sunk an eclipse that shades our real selves.

Virginia, to her utter surprise, seemed almost apologetic as she said, "I am sorry for the remark about you in regards to your bold rhetoric. It was a tasteless remark. Whatever induced me to make it, I can't think. Getting foolish in my old age, I suppose."

Jesus replied, "Surely you are not old."

"I'm thirty-nine in a couple of months," snapped out Virginia, surprised that she would admit her age. "You don't call it young I suppose?"

"I think it a beautiful age," insisted Jesus. "Young enough not to have lost the joy of youth, but old enough to have learned much that elevates the joy of life."

"It can be a trying time of life."

Jesus offered, "It can; I suppose. It is said that the old believe everything, the middle aged suspect everything and the young know everything."

"Oh, I daresay," returned Cap Johnson, "I can tell by your demeanour that you believe any age is beautiful. That seems the kind of person you are."

WHEN JESUS CAME TO LADYSMITH
TO BATTLE THE ANGEL OF DEATH

"Age is just a number, nothing more," replied Jesus."

Ileana was impatient to have a look at herself in the mirror in her own room with the door shut, because she suddenly felt beautiful and needed to actually look at herself in private. She rose and said, "Goodnight."

Jesus gave her a knowing nod, got up and strolled towards the bookshelf, seeking something to read.

"You seem to have frightened away Ileana," remarked the one man who had seemed disinterested from the start and had sat quietly reading the newspaper. He was the only one who had not encountered Jesus earlier. He was a retired naval officer awaiting the building of his home high on a mountain overlooking the bay. It just so happened he was Commander Ray, the man who had been visited days earlier by Calvin Hobbs, the American chargé d'affaires in Victoria.

"It seems that is so" admitted Jesus, as he continued, "I have not had the pleasure of an introduction."

"I am Commodore Ray, retired, and I assume you are the man calling himself Jesus."

"I am he, indeed."

WHEN JESUS CAME TO LADYSMITH
TO BATTLE THE ANGEL OF DEATH

"Why," asked a smug Commodore, "would you call yourself that?"

"It is the name given me by my mother, and I would not dishonour such a fine person by changing it," offered Jesus as he removed a book and walked by to his chair.

Cavalierly, the commodore said, "And I suppose her name was Mary?"

"Ironically," replied Jesus, "that was her name, and I can even top that."

"How?"

"My father's name was Joseph."

All there tried to restrain laughter as the commodore said, "And you probably had a cousin named John."

"Yes, he was a French Cajun, named John Baptise," offered Jesus with a cheshire grin.

Some could not restrain their laughter, and giggled out loud, but Jesus was used to this type of reaction to his name and said, "A good name should be carried with dignity, because names have power. They can be uttered in pride, in respect, in awe, in appreciation and at their worst they can be uttered with contempt."

WHEN JESUS CAME TO LADYSMITH
TO BATTLE THE ANGEL OF DEATH

The commodore was affected by this man's obvious self-respect and intensity of purpose, but he wondered what that purpose was, and why he had chosen this particular place to reside. The commodore, despite being imbued with bravery along with a cavalier disregard for decency, felt, for the first time ever, a tinge of fear when he looked at the man calling himself Jesus. Why did he fear him? Primarily he feared this man because he had been preparing for the particular mission he was currently on for many years. Building a new home on the mountain was nothing more than a cover for his real intent, an intent that included a search for something that would alter the course of history, something that would shake the foundations of a somewhat ordered world, something that would be an earthquake of evil the magnitude of which had never occurred before. It would rock the foundations of the earth, and here was a man named Jesus showing up to, perhaps, throw a gigantic cog in the machinery that had been set in motion by nefarious forces.

The commodore was tall, muscular, white but with a definite tinge of blackness to his skin not born of ethnicity, but of a dark soul that enjoyed watching people suffer indignities in the darkness of evil, he was the serpent coiled to strike, ever vigilant in search of a victim, lurking in the shadows, staring with wide eyes black as inky pools, hardened features, immobile face, gaunt, hair slicked back, deep furrows under protruding

J. Wayne Frye

cheek bones, evil glint in the eyes, slow almost orchestrated movements of his hands while he flexed as if he had no bones at all. He was a slinking, oozing, false smiling creature about to turn on the suddenly friendly false charm – a despicable charm meant to disarm any who stood in the way of his mission.

Shifting in his chair, the commodore sarcastically said, "A charming family I am sure, since you are such a charming fellow."

Realizing the sarcasm in the statement by the commodore, a knowing smile creased Jesus' lips as he responded. "Oh, thank you for the compliment, but charm is often illusionary. My mother was indeed a woman of charming character, and my father, who was a carpenter, was equally charming. However, both my parents were much meeker than I am. I do not believe it is the meek who will inherit the earth, but rather, it has currently been inherited by the bombastic, crude captains of commerce who believe people are nothing but commodities to be used up and then discarded when they are no longer useful. Countering the evil of the capitalist oppressors will not be accomplished by meekly asking for your rights. Rather, you must demand them. Being meek before those who look upon you as chattel accomplishes absolutely nothing. That is just a sign to the powerful and privileged that the masses are weak and unwilling to fight for a cause.

WHEN JESUS CAME TO LADYSMITH
TO BATTLE THE ANGEL OF DEATH

Unfortunately, most people are willing to be slaves, because they are propagandized into believing they are free."

"A rather narrowly defined cryptically cynical outlook on things I'd say," interjected Cap Johnson.

Jesus, in a calm, authoritative voice replied, "Cynical? Yes, I am cynical, because I have watched for so many years how people refuse to stand against the tyranny of the ruling class. Today's world is no different than the feudal system where the lords of the manor held peasants in bondage to the land. Today, people are in bondage to corporations upon whom they are dependent for a job. They have been brainwashed into believing that happiness is a commodity that can be bought and sold. The wealthy and the corporations are the modern equivalent of the lords of the manor. One percent of the population controls eighty percent of the wealth, and governments represent them, not the struggling masses."

"That is the way of the world since its inception," said Marie Kemp.

"It is the way of the world," replied Jesus, "because of the complacency of the masses that have been oppressed so long they have lost the will to fight."

WHEN JESUS CAME TO LADYSMITH
TO BATTLE THE ANGEL OF DEATH

Cap Johnson's wife, shifting about in her chair, said, "The people who are in power have no interest in us. We vote, but nothing changes, because we don't have the money and influence to facilitate change."

"I have interest in you," Jesus assured her. "And you may assume I have no power, because I have no money, but I have the power of my voice, the power of my kindness and dedication, but more importantly, I have the same power that Che Guevara, the greatest revolutionary to ever draw breath, had. Che was an atheist, but he did more to help the poor, more to lift up the downtrodden, the oppressed, the persecuted and distressed than any minister who ever stood in the pulpit pleading with people to accept their fate, because there will be a reward in the hereafter. Che made no promises of the hereafter, but he promised people they could control their own fate through activism by standing up to authority, standing up to those who enslaved them. That is why he had to be killed. Like that revolutionary who walked the Middle East so many years ago, he and so many others had to be crucified for the gravest sin in the capitalist system – the sin of challenging the economic slavery that traps people in bondage to the moneyed class. Evil is at the very root of a system that allows people to go without sustenance, while others dine on the fatted calf in their lavish palaces of excess that reek of moral decay."

WHEN JESUS CAME TO LADYSMITH
TO BATTLE THE ANGEL OF DEATH

Those there were enthralled by the elegance of this simple man; all that is but Commodore Ray, as he looked suspiciously at Jesus, seemingly with disgust. Yet, within his eyes was a twinkling that signified fear.

J. Wayne Frye

Chapter 5
A Creature from Hell

I want you tumbling
Through the darkness.
I want you to hear the thud,
When you hit the bottom.

I want you to hear the shutter,
Not the applause and cheers.
I don't want the truth.
I want glorious lies.
..................The Devil

Calvin Hobbs seemed almost exhausted after his
tale about finding a man with a hole in his chest
and his heart missing. He eased back in his chair.

WHEN JESUS CAME TO LADYSMITH
TO BATTLE THE ANGEL OF DEATH

Aaron said, "You surely have more to share? I need more details. What I have now is nothing but the fact Mr. Hobbs that you found a body with the heart missing, but I need to know more about what happened afterward."

Taking a deep breath, Hobbs offered, "Oh, yes, I do have more to share, definitely."

Clarence Manly said, "What Hobbs has related is accurate. He is the only one who was there, so none of us can verify his veracity based on observing the incident, but we have no reason to doubt him. He is an honourable man."

"Now," said Hobbs, "the truth is I was as frightened as I ever had been in my entire life. I was wondering what was going on upstairs, as I was told someone would be coming down. I had heard sombre music and loud chanting while outside, but there was no one about, only the man who had been sitting on the bench, and perhaps someone he called 'the angel.' I walked into the hallway and looked down at a backdoor to the house, and I assumed everyone had perhaps left by the back way, which would have explained what happened to them all."

"You say you were lost. Why not just use your GPS on your cell-phone?"

"I had left it at the hotel," replied Hobbs.

WHEN JESUS CAME TO LADYSMITH
TO BATTLE THE ANGEL OF DEATH

"A plausible explanation I suppose. Since the old flip phones went out of vogue, the ones you could attach to your belt, I often do the same. Of course, at my age, forgetfulness is a more normal occurrence than it used to be."

"True for me also, but I have a suspicion that even if I had my phone it would not have worked. There was something inexplicably strange and sinister about what was going on, something that seemed to be of an almost supernatural nature."

"Perhaps you should go on about what happened once this so-called angel showed up."

"That's just it," replied Hobbs as he took a long, deep breath. "The man who went to get the angel, whatever that meant, never came down."

"Really?"

"Yes."

"So, what did you do then? Did you not go upstairs to look for them?"

"No, absolutely not, Mr. Adams. Why would I ever, in a million years, do that? As much as I am ashamed to admit it, I was too scared. I walked into the hallway, looked up the stairs and what I saw at the top of those stairs convinced me to scurry away."

WHEN JESUS CAME TO LADYSMITH
TO BATTLE THE ANGEL OF DEATH

"And what did you see? Be as descriptive as possible."

"There, at the top of the stairs, was an undulating figure with dark, partially flapping, huge bird-like wings extending from its back. I saw its glowing eyes in the shadows. The angel of death was there at the top of the stairs, and I was about to die. It was tall, thin, pale as death, pale as the full moon, pale as the chalk in a teacher's hand, vigilant-like, menacingly lurking, staring like a cobra seeking its prey, wide eyes black as inky pools, dark shadows under deeply sunken eyes, hardened features, immobile face, gaunt, hair long and scraggily, deep darkness under protruding cheek bones, evil glint in the glaring stare, movements as if in slow motion, slinking, oozing with evil. I felt, standing there at the bottom of the stairs, like I had descended into a dark pit, an abyss of agony. I was in hell. The thing's emaciated left-hand fingers were clenched tightly on what seemed to be a scythe. A scythe covered with blood stains, each one telling a different story of how this manifestation, this abomination, this evil had decapitated the breath of life. Looking at the bloody blade of the scythe, staring intently at the pointed, curved edge I realized it could be used to cut open a chest and remove a heart. That is when I turned and dashed for the door, never looking back to see if that thing was behind me. I fumbled for the door knob, desperately trying to get out of the den of evil, that

104 **J. Wayne Frye**

place of terror like I had never encountered before. I escaped or did I?"

Hobbs again eased back in his overstuffed chair, and contemplatively continued, "I felt as if I had gazed upon the emperor of death, but still there was a sadness in those haunting, penetrating eyes. Had he lifted up his brow against his maker and been cast from heaven? Had he experienced the tribulation of evil himself? The thing seemed to almost regret its wickedness. Maybe it was sorry for what it appeared forced to do, as if it had no choice but to do evil. Was he as fair once as he now was foul? Those thoughts ran through my head as I leaped onto the porch and down the walkway. I fumbled to open the gate and bounded onto the sidewalk. I then turned to look back at the house and what I saw astounded me."

Aaron interrupted him. "The house undulating."

"How did you know?"

"It is obvious Mr. Hobbs. Sounds like the whole affair was a hallucination."

"Oh no; it was no hallucination."

"Had you drank with your friend at the boarding house?"

"The commodore does not drink."

WHEN JESUS CAME TO LADYSMITH
TO BATTLE THE ANGEL OF DEATH

Aaron contemplated for a few seconds and said, "And when you were on the sidewalk, looked back and saw the undulating house I assume that the fog had lifted?"

"It had, yes. Only a slight misty fog was left. I seemed to come back to reality and proceeded down the empty street to my accommodations, where I fell into a deep sleep."

A contemplative tone to his voice, Aaron said, "So you told the police the story exactly as you have told me."

"Yes, exactly."

"Of course," offered Aaron, "they assumed you were intoxicated."

"They did, but they also decided that I was entitled to be heard out, probably because of my position. Had I been without influence, I am sure they would have ignored me."

"Of course they would have," offered Aaron. "The police are supposed to serve the affluent and influential. Their real purpose is to keep the peons in line, to protect the affluent in their gated estates from the peasants. That is the way it always has been."

"Poppycock!" shouted Dr. Borden.

WHEN JESUS CAME TO LADYSMITH
TO BATTLE THE ANGEL OF DEATH

"Poppycock?" replied Aaron, his voice rising. "The police were not created to protect and serve the population. They were not created to stop real crime, because if they stopped real crime the jails would be full of bankers and Wall Street tycoons. And they were certainly not created to promote justice. They were created to protect wage-slave capitalism that requires the wealthy to keep the working class in line and protect their privileged status. The police are a form apart. Why do you think they wear uniforms? That militarizes them and is meant to instil fear in the working class. There was a never a time when the police neutrally enforced the law. The police use violence to deal with the social problems that accompany the development of a slave-labour economy. Look at the USA, and you see the epicentre of this culture of service to the affluent. George Floyd with a cop's knee on his throat for nine minutes choking the life out of him and the countless other people who have been slaughtered under the jack-booted Gestapo mentality get no justice, because justice is an ideal but not a reality. I am a realist, and you, Mr. Hobbs, will get more service than most, because of your affluence and station in life, but I learned long ago to never expect too much from police. However, you are lucky to be in Canada, and the RCMP is far superior to the American Gestapo when it comes to justice and serving the interest of the less-affluent. Still, you left something out, maybe just by chance."

J. Wayne Frye   107

WHEN JESUS CAME TO LADYSMITH
TO BATTLE THE ANGEL OF DEATH

A puzzled look on his face, Calvin Hobbs said, "No, I left nothing out."

"Are you 100% sure?"

Taking a deep breath, he replied. "No, nothing."

"What time did you leave Commodore Ray?"

"It was about 9:30 PM."

"And you walked about two kilometres to where the house was."

"Yes, about that."

"I can walk a kilometre in about ten minutes. We are close to the same age. How long does it take you to walk a kilometre?"

"About the same."

"So, twenty to thirty minutes tops for two kilometres then to where you entered the house, right?"

"Sure."

"Did you by any chance check your watch after you found yourself outside the house?"

"Yes, as I was walking toward my hotel."

WHEN JESUS CAME TO LADYSMITH
TO BATTLE THE ANGEL OF DEATH

"The time?"

"11:15."

Very sternly, Aaron said, "So, you were in the house for how long?"

"Ten minutes tops."

"Assuming you got to the house around 10:00, based upon 20 to 30 minutes walking time after leaving the commodore's at 9:30, and ten minutes at the house, it should have been 10:10 or 10:15. How to you explain the one hour difference in the time?"

Everyone there was astounded that no one, not even the police lieutenant who spoke to them, was observant enough to come up with the time differential. Aaron said, "So, it is obvious there is one hour you cannot account for. Where were you and what happened?"

Mystified, all there stared blankly as Hobbs said, "So, you are saying I lost an entire hour somewhere, somehow?"

"Seems that is the case."

Taking a deep breath and then slowly exhaling, Hobbs said, "But how could that happen? It does not make sense."

WHEN JESUS CAME TO LADYSMITH
TO BATTLE THE ANGEL OF DEATH

"I have found through thousands of cases that things often do not make sense. It is sometimes my job to make sense of the nonsensical. That is how I earn my money, and I will take this case."

All there seemed relieved to know that they had just found a champion for their cause, a man known for his dogged determination and unflinching devotion to finding the truth.

Hobbs said, "I am so grateful, because this has all of us so bewildered."

Aaron said, "Now, there might be some things you may have unintentionally left out. You mentioned you had dinner at a place called Jack's. You passed by it on your way back to your hotel, right?"

"I did, yes."

"Was it open at that time?"

"Yes, as well as I remember they close at midnight."

"You do not remember having gone in?"

"Did not go in, no."

"We will go there and make some inquiries. I do not doubt you, but I think it prudent to see if, for

J. Wayne Frye

some unknown reason, you might have gone in, and blocked it from your memory. Stranger things have happened. My partner, Chablis (pronounced Sha-blee) Louise Chavez, once had a case where a man committed a murder and completely blocked it from his memory. Sometimes the workings of the mind are beyond explanation."

"I am at your disposal."

Charles Porter slowly and methodically, almost as if contrived, bent forward, and looking directly at Aaron said, "Gotta go, my grandson is visiting. The cat's in the cradle."

Hearing the lines "the cat's in the cradle" reminded Aaron where he had seen Porter before. He looked up at him and said, "You were once a singer. I heard you in a club down in Greenwich Village. You were good, especially when you sang "The Cat's in the Cradle."

Smiling, Porter said, "Yep, I was pretty good, but my singing career fizzled out, and I got into politics and you know I lost a wife and a child because I had no time for 'um. Gotta a grandson now, which is why I am in Ladysmith. Not gonna make the same mistake I did with my son. Time is the most precious commodity any of us have. Good luck to you and Hobbs. Hope you get to the bottom of this," and as he left he was softly singing to himself, "Cat's in the Cradle."

WHEN JESUS CAME TO LADYSMITH
TO BATTLE THE ANGEL OF DEATH

My child arrived just the other day.
He came to the world in the usual way.
But there were planes to catch, and bills to pay.
He learned to walk while I was away.
And he was talking 'fore I knew it, and as he grew
He'd say "I'm gonna be like you, dad.
You know I'm gonna be like you."

And the cat's in the cradle and the silver spoon,
Little boy blue and the man in the moon.
"When you coming home, dad?"
I replied, "I don't know when,
But we'll get together then.
You know we'll have a good time then."

My son turned ten just the other day.
Said, "thanks for the ball, dad, come on let's play.
Can you teach me to throw," I said, "not today;
I got a lot to do." He said, "That's okay,"
And he walked away, but his smile never dimmed.
It said, "I'm gonna be like him, yeah.
You know I'm gonna be like him."

And the cat's in the cradle and the silver spoon,
Little boy blue and the man in the moon.
"When you coming home, dad?"
I replied, "I don't know when,
But we'll get together then.
You know we'll have a good time then."

Well, he came from college just the other day.
So much like a man I just had to say,

J. Wayne Frye

WHEN JESUS CAME TO LADYSMITH
TO BATTLE THE ANGEL OF DEATH

"Son, I'm proud of you, can you sit for a while?"
He shook his head, and he said with a smile,
"What I'd really like is to borrow the car keys.
See you later, can I have them please?"

And the cat's in the cradle and the silver spoon,
Little boy blue and the man in the moon.
"When you coming home, dad?"
I replied, "I don't know when,
But we'll get together then.
You know we'll have a good time then."

I've long since retired and my son's moved away.
I called him up just the other day.
I said, "I'd like to see you if you don't mind."
He said, "I'd love to, dad, if I could find the time.
My new job's a hassle, and the kids have the flu.
But it's sure nice talking to you, dad.
It's been sure nice talking to you."

And as I hung up the phone, it occurred to me
He'd grown up just like me.
My boy was just like me.
And the cat's in the cradle and the silver spoon,
Little boy blue and the man in the moon.
"When you coming home, dad?"
I replied, "I don't know when,
But we'll get together then.
You know we'll have a good time then."

Songwriters: Sandy Chapin / Harry F. Chapin
Cat's in the Cradle lyrics © Warner Chappell Music, Inc

J. Wayne Frye   113

WHEN JESUS CAME TO LADYSMITH
TO BATTLE THE ANGEL OF DEATH

Looking at Porter walk out stooped shouldered, as if he was carrying a heavy burden made Aaron reflect back on his childhood, and his own father who never had time for him. Mistakes made in relationships are the burdens that we carry to the grave. Lost opportunities, lost possibilities that we can never recover are in a storage room of regrets. That is part of what it means to realize that so much of life is wasted on things that do not really matter. Inside our brains there is a giant file of sacred lost moments and solemn missed opportunities where the past haunts us. Aaron, even as an old man, still harboured the agony of not feeling like his father loved him. He could understand the misery, the pain and the woe of Charles Porter; because Aaron knew his own father had been guilty of the same thing. Aaron displayed a tough exterior, but within, he had a heart that beat with the rhythm of compassion. He took a deep breath and said to Hobbs, "Let's walk over to Jack's."

At that very moment, Hobbs, despite his concerns over seeing a dead man that was not found by the authorities and even the house where he had sent the authorities to investigate did not apparently exist, seemed excited that the most celebrated private detective in North America was going to tackle the case. What they were going to find out at Jack's he did not know, but his respect for Aaron's deductive acumen made him hopeful that an answer was possible.

J. Wayne Frye

WHEN JESUS CAME TO LADYSMITH
TO BATTLE THE ANGEL OF DEATH

As they left the club Aaron asked if there was anything in Hobbs' life the past few days or maybe weeks or months that seemed out of the ordinary, besides the events that night in the fog, of course, things of even a very private nature that might have some bearing on what happened.

"Well, I have not been a saint; although, I have never been overtly perverse in my romantic pursuits. I have always been aware of my public image, so there have been some times when I have made sure to be discreet in my private life. Recently though, I cannot think of anything in particular."

Aaron could see that there was something Hobbs was holding back, so he said, "I am a discreet person, and I never reveal anything my clients share about their lives, as the bond between a private investigator and the client is as sacrosanct as that between a lawyer and a client."

Hobbs contemplated for awhile until he finally said, "Maybe, I am not sure, but let me share what may be something strange. I am a member of the small American contingent here on the island. In Victoria, I, for three days, spent time with a well-known American businessman named Lloyd Edison, who was terribly ill and at the point of death. Two physicians were flown in from the USA to attend him and they required special diplomatic dispensation to do so; consequently, I got involved, as he felt too important to go to the hospital, where in Canada, all people get the same treatment from a Prime Minister to a janitor. He felt his financial status somehow made him worthy of special consideration. I am sure you know how rich Americans think they should get the very best treatment available based on a system of class distinction in the USA that is not as prevalent here in Canada."

"The USA," replied Aaron "is one of the great bastions of class distinction. They fought a war to free themselves of servitude to royalty, but they have instituted their own form of royalty – the rich. Everything revolves around the accumulation of wealth, and the peasant class has been brainwashed into believing everyone has an equal chance at success. That absurdity is promoted by the privileged class to convince the average person that they too can be a part of the elite. That explains why a buffoon like Trump wound up as President, put into office by the very people he had great disdain for under the assumption they were from an inferior gene pool. It is amazing how the unthinking masses can be deluded into voting against their own best interests. But go on with your tale about the wealthy American, as it may have some relation to what occurred."

"By the hour he seemed to grow weaker; but although his bodily strength was apparently leaving him, his mind remained clear and active.

WHEN JESUS CAME TO LADYSMITH
TO BATTLE THE ANGEL OF DEATH

Late one day word was received at our office that he wished his lawyer to be summoned at once from Los Angeles and to bring with him certain papers. It was highly unusual for us to get involved in such a matter, but when it comes to the wealthy, I am afraid that we are at their beckoning call. What these papers were is not essential; I mention them only to explain how it was that a few nights ago I happened to be at Lloyd Edison's bedside."

The two arrived at Jack's, went in, took a seat at a table by the window fronting First Avenue and ordered drinks, as Hobbs continued. "The lawyer, Nick Beale, took a private plane to the Victoria Airport, arriving in only a few hours. I met him, and we immediately went to Lloyd Edison's home. He was sleeping, and the attending private physician whom he had flown in from Seattle refused to have him awakened. Beale urged that he should be allowed to receive Edison's instructions concerning certain documents, but the physician would not disturb him as he needed his rest. So, we all gathered in the library to wait until he should awake of his own accord. It was about one o'clock in the morning, while we were still there, that Chief Inspector Lyle and two other officers from the local RCMP detachment came to talk to Edison in regards to the murder of his brother. You can imagine our dismay and distress. His brother, Robert Edison, had been assumed to be in England on business, but was, in fact, found on a deserted beach in the Oak Bay area of Victoria, stabbed to death with a large serrated dagger of some sort. "

"Now, with the police insisting to see Lloyd Edison, we went into Edison's bedroom and awoke him. He seemed totally unconcerned about his brother's death, and there was a heated exchange between him and the officers. In typical privileged person fashion, he ordered the police to get out of his house or face the wrath of the U.S. government on his behalf. The officers all left without asking any questions. You see, in almost any country of the world, wealthy Americans are feared. Their arrogance is legendary, as they project an image of entitlement that puts them above the ordinary people who must cower in fear before the law."

Aaron interjected, "That is the way of the world that always allows for deference to Americans, a world where Americans are not respected but feared. Every country fears the wrath of the USA, because they all need the economic benefits offered by the most corrupt nation on earth, a nation that has no moral core. You, as a diplomat, know that, but would never admit it, because, like most of us, you fear not being able to put food on the table. In the blink of an eye, your very existence can be eradicated by the cruellest economic system ever devised, a system that knows no restraint when it comes to greed."

WHEN JESUS CAME TO LADYSMITH
TO BATTLE THE ANGEL OF DEATH

"You are a most perceptive man when it comes to the economic factors that make prisoners of 99% of the human race, Mr. Adams. Of course you are right, but I could never openly admit it out of fear I would be out on the street looking for a job."

"I understand that," replied Aaron. "And what of Edison's condition?"

"Medical condition? Oh, he looked completely healed of any malady. He was incredibly robust."

Aaron could tell that there was something that had suddenly occurred to Hobbs, something he had apparently forgotten until that very moment. Aaron said, "What is it?"

"I just realized something which I noticed on that night in the bedroom, something that was incredibly strange."

"Yes?" quizzically replied Aaron.

"As I was leaving, walking out the door of the bedroom, I looked over at the far balcony sliding glass door overlooking the bay. The night was very dark as clouds had covered a full moon. It was so dark that you could almost feel the darkness wrapping itself around you, luring you into a horrid pit, a pit that wanted to trap you in blackness, wanted to bore itself into your consciousness. No, bore its way into the subconscious."

Ever astute, Aaron said, "But there was something else. I can see it in your eyes."

Sighing, Hobbs replied, "The clouds had passed over the moon just as I was closing the door, and the moonlight glowed down upon the balcony floor, and there I saw the shadow of a horrid creature, the shadow I now realize I saw again in that house on the foggy night. Oh, what a horrible shadow of an entity that seemed to be from the depths of evil. It was a thing – a horrid thing with flapping wings hiding out of sight in the corner of the balcony. I blotted it from my memory. Oh, how do you battle against a creature from hell?"

WHEN JESUS CAME TO LADYSMITH
TO BATTLE THE ANGEL OF DEATH

Chapter 6
He Who Stands Against Evil

Enlightenment is like the sun.
It warms the soul of mankind.
It makes the tyranny and oppressions
Of mind and body vanish
Like evil spirits at the dawn of day.

Ileana Rabe and Virginia Davis had left, but returned together for some reason to take a seat with the rest there in the drawing room. Jesus smiled at Ileana, and intentionally ignored the haughty Virginia Davis, because he wanted to let her know that beauty alone did not make you attractive. People are like stained glass windows. They sparkle and shine when the sun is out, but when the darkness sets in their true beauty is revealed only if there is a light from within, and Jesus could see that there was no light from within Virginia Davis. She lived in fear of the day when her beauty would be gone.

Still looking at Ileana, Jesus said, "You are very vibrant looking tonight. You shine a wonderful light of gayety in the room."

Virginia got a scowl on her face, as she was obviously offended that someone would take notice of a woman whom she felt lacked grace and savior-faire when compared to her. She was unable, in her self-absorption, to understand that jealousy was hatred built upon insecurity.

"It is very kind of you to say so," offered Ileana, "but I am afraid you are in need of some glasses when looking at me."

"Never underestimate your value in making other people's lives better with a smile. True beauty is initiated from within not from without. You would be surprised at how valuable a smile can be to people lost in the struggles of every day life."

"I am afraid you overvalue my worth, dear sir."

"Your gentle face, your gentle voice, your gentle bearing all proclaim your value."

J. Wayne Frye

WHEN JESUS CAME TO LADYSMITH
TO BATTLE THE ANGEL OF DEATH

Virginia was fuming with inner rage, but that was what Jesus intended. He wanted her, without directly telling her, to look within herself and see that she should not rely on physical beauty alone, because her worth was not in her physical appearance, but in her power to be compassionate. Beauty is a commodity that fades with time, but the beauty of compassion always trumps physical beauty, and if properly nourished will last a lifetime.

Virginia looked without flinching into Jesus' eyes, and gradually a smile banished the reigning dullness of her features. She, after so many years, realized that people whose opinion really mattered judge you by what you are, not by the way you look."

Jesus remained silent, but looked into Virginia's eyes as if to say, "Welcome to reality, and welcome to a new world where you will find your real worth to people based on your heart not your physical appearance."

Just then, Cap Johnson's wife said, "Physical appearance has a lot to do with how we are accepted. I dress in a fine manner to convey that I respect myself. That way others can respect me, too. I deplore people who have so little self-respect that they dress in tattered jeans, obscene clothing that exposes too much flesh or flaunt their bodies in other grotesque ways."

WHEN JESUS CAME TO LADYSMITH
TO BATTLE THE ANGEL OF DEATH

"Life," replied a calm voiced Jesus, "is not about how many clothes you have or how much they cost. It's about the lives you touch and the love and respect you show those who cannot afford fine clothes, nice cars or luxurious mansions. Your clothes look very nice Mrs. Johnson, and I compliment you on your taste, but I would be as complimentary to a dirty clothed homeless individual who shares his meagre meal with a fellow person who is down and out. Clothes have nothing to do with the respect you should get. Clothes do not make the person. The compassionate person, regardless of what he or she is wearing, makes a statement about their humanity. Compassion elevates anyone to a kingly or queenly regal appearance in my eyes."

Mrs. Johnson took a long deep breath and realized that she had just been put in her place by a skilled technician of subtlety. She said, "There is something very curious in your nature that gets to the heart of a matter. I seem quite unable to avoid insulting myself, which I have just done. Of course, I think you may have insulted my way of thinking, and to you sir I say touché."

Flabbergasted by bewilderment, she wished Jesus good-night, hoping when next they met she would be more pleasant, more able to be the person she should be. Jesus gave her a generous smile, and through his silence conveyed an appreciation of her metamorphous in thought.

J. Wayne Frye

WHEN JESUS CAME TO LADYSMITH
TO BATTLE THE ANGEL OF DEATH

Cap Johnson got up and left with his wife, looking at Jesus on the way out with a kind of knowing nod, as if to say, "Thanks for enlightening my wife."

"Tell me," laughed Diane Jenks, "how do you manage to get to the very heart of a matter the way you do."

"I have had years of experience in showing people a better path I suppose, and I can see the innate goodness others cannot."

"Tell me," asked Diane Jenks, "something that worries me about you."

"I will if I can," replied Jesus.

"Where are you from and why are you here?"

"I am from nowhere and from everywhere. I suppose one would call me a vagabond, because I roam about the land always in search of a way to lift those low in spirit and to encourage those put upon by a society based on greed to fight for justice. It is a lonely battle, a battle mostly lost, because people are too complacent to rise up against their own slavery. I also, sometimes, am called upon to battle the angels of blackness that manifest themselves in ways few people can imagine. I stand against the darkness that blots out the light of hope."

J. Wayne Frye 125

WHEN JESUS CAME TO LADYSMITH
TO BATTLE THE ANGEL OF DEATH

Mary Jenks was in awe of Jesus, and sat enthralled listening to him seemingly reach deep within her mother and find something that had been lost so long ago. She looked at her mother, and for the first time in years they smiled at each other with genuine affection.

"It is a pleasure," said Jesus, "to observe a mother and daughter, both of whom are so extraordinarily devoted to one another."

Both mother and daughter knew that they had lost that vital connection so long ago, but in the presence of this simple man, who was actually lying to elevate their appreciation of one another they felt a rekindling of what had disappeared in the most monumental of all struggles called life. Life's trials weighted people down, stooped their shoulders with burdens which society should help alleviate, but selfishness and governments in service to the elite had cast aside compassion for the vast majority of people who lived lives of quiet desperation.

Diane Jenks said, "You are a mastermind of subtle manipulation."

"No," replied Jesus. "I am a master of finding the goodness in people, finding that which is often hidden deep within. That which people are afraid to let surface out of fear they will be misjudged or misunderstood."

WHEN JESUS CAME TO LADYSMITH
TO BATTLE THE ANGEL OF DEATH

Mary Jenks said, "You can read faces, too, can't you?"

"Perhaps I can, yes. For example, with you I see a beautiful and interesting face that shows you have great courage."

Mary offered, "Courage? That is something I have always lacked."

Smiling, Jesus said, 'Most ordinary people must muster great courage to get through every single day. The vast majority of people in a world where poverty and struggle are the result of an economic system skewed toward the privileged have extraordinary courage of the most profound kind. Survival in that kind of world is a daunting task. Greed, vanity and sordidness are always looking for victims to trap in the whirlpool of evil. Yet, I see in your angelic face an almost fierce scorn of lies, scorn of hypocrisy. I see the desire for all things pure and abhorrence of all things that are contemptible."

I wonder, postulated Mary, is that why those others hurried from the room? Did they feel ashamed of the littleness that had been apparent in them when looked at by those clear, believing eyes of this incredible man? Her black eyes brightly flashed with heartfelt tenderness upon him, and meeting his gaze, she smiled at him affectionately.

WHEN JESUS CAME TO LADYSMITH
TO BATTLE THE ANGEL OF DEATH

"Nothing, so it seems to me," said Jesus, "is more beautiful than the love that has weathered the storms of life. You and your mother obviously have that kind of love. The sweet, tender blossom that flowers in the heart of the young; in hearts such as yours is beautiful. The love of the young for the old, that is the essence of life, for the elderly as well as the young crave love, and I can see your abiding love for your mother."

Diane Jenks was near tears now, fighting back the urge to start bawling. She realized all the wrong done her daughter, realized that she had taken out the harshness of her life, her predicament on someone who deserved better. She said to Jesus in a trembling voice, "You seem to find all things beautiful."

"Not necessarily, because there is much ugliness in the world, but the beautiful trumps the ugly if people look deep within and find that spark of compassion we are all capable of. Well, most of us are capable of, because there are those dark spirits among us that get pleasure in evil, in hatred, in depravity and in debauchery."

Commodore Ray said, "You three are having a very absorbing conversation." He rose and in a playful mood laid his hand upon Jesus' shoulder, an action that necessitated his looking straight into Jesus' eyes. Ray turned scarlet. Jesus' lips did not move, but the commodore could read his thoughts.

WHEN JESUS CAME TO LADYSMITH
TO BATTLE THE ANGEL OF DEATH

The impression remaining was not to be shaken off. He felt the disdain sear his flesh. He turned and walked out of the room without uttering another word.

Jesus had arrived at the Jenks Boarding House with its seemingly commonplace, mean-minded, coarse-fibred occupants absorbed in themselves and their individual miseries. Yet, in the course of one evening the tenor, because of Jesus, was coming round to reflect a greater depth of compassion and appreciation for life.

Mrs. Jenks and her daughter had reconnected with understanding and love for one another. And through it all, mousy Marie Kemp had sat without uttering a word. To her, Jesus was a witty and delightful conversationalist with a most attractive personality. If Marie Kemp had one failing, it was lack of vanity. She was unaware of her own delicate and refined beauty. If she could only see herself with his, the stranger's eyes, the modesty that rendered her distrustful of her natural charms would fall from her. When Jesus turned toward her, looking straight into her eyes, she was in awe of his mesmerizing powerful gaze.

The commodore said to Cap Johnson in the upstairs hallway, "I have met that miscreant rebel-rouser before in different places in different forms. He is that perennial do-gooder who is always demonstrating for an improvement in society, an improvement in the human condition, a condition that needs no improvement. These malcontents are always marching about something, when what they need to do is shut up and find a job rather than always finding fault. I wish to goodness he would go, because he is intent on wrecking havoc on this peaceful place."

Jesus' belief in the innate goodness of most people he came across was abhorrent to the commodore, a man harbouring a deep secret that would soon be unleashed on an unsuspecting Ladysmith. He was an ageing man who was representative of that world where change is frightening to those in positions of privilege, because change opened up opportunity, and fighting change was what the establishment did best, because the establishment feared change.

Virginia Davis lay on her bed in her usual seductive state of nakedness staring at the ceiling, reflecting on the sleek, luxury-loving self she was who had so often been quite willing to sell herself to the highest bidder who could offer her the finest clothes, the richest foods, the most sumptuous surroundings. Such a current bidder was a local banker with a wife and three children, an exceedingly rich rotund old gentleman. So fond of her was the banker that he had put her up in the boarding house with promises that one day he would buy her a nice home where she could live in luxury as his mistress. She had been patiently waiting for three months now, meeting him clandestinely three times a week at a motel in a nearby town. She shivered in shame thinking about how she had so willingly sacrificed her integrity for the promise of a life of luxurious splendour from a man she secretly found despicable. Her dark, alluring eyes teared up, as she reflected on what Jesus had so aptly said to her downstairs. She actually was ashamed of herself, but what could she do? She was exceedingly beautiful, but had absolutely no marketable skills. She had always used her beauty to lure men into providing for her, but she had never found one who loved her enough to put a ring on her finger. She suddenly realized that perhaps her beauty was more a detriment than an asset. After all, she was aging now, and the days were numbered when she could rely on her beauty as a meal ticket. She began to sob, thinking that maybe Jesus would embrace her with love, but what did he have to offer? He was poor and a vagabond. And here it was that the stranger's opinion of her not only irritated but inconvenienced her. Under the very eyes of a person, however foolish, convinced that you are possessed of all the highest attributes of your sex, it is difficult to behave as though actuated by only the basest motives. The stranger would one day depart. Indeed, he had told her himself that he was but a passing traveller. When he was gone it would be easier for her to return to acceptance of her old life and not feel even a tinge of guilt.

WHEN JESUS CAME TO LADYSMITH
TO BATTLE THE ANGEL OF DEATH

In fact, she actually imagined Jesus one afternoon entering her room where she would stand by the window, looking out upon the street below. It would be just another foggy fall afternoon. No one else would be in the room. The strange man would gently knock on the door and she would say, "Enter." He would do so, closing the door, and come towards her with that curious, almost slow motion stride of his. He would tell her good-bye and she would ask if she might see him again, but he would say, "perhaps, but I doubt it."

The thought of him leaving had her now experiencing tears raining from her eyes. She shivered at the thought of not seeing him again. No man had ever affected her like this. Why? Why was she shedding profuse tears over a man who was not even physically appealing to her? Why was she attracted to him the way she was. It had nothing to do with sex. It was more a soulful attraction, an attraction to his simplicity, to his goodness.

One does not live on love in the cruel world Virginia had let drive a stake though her soul. She had fixed her sights on men with money and the things that money can buy. She thought about her banker lover with disdain now. He was a slimy pig of a man who stole more with the stroke of a pen than a robber stole with a gun. He was a despicable human being with no depth of character but with the money she craved to somehow make her feel safe in a world that was filled with all kinds of demons wrecking havoc on those who always seemed to be on the outside looking in. She was growing old, and had many penniless suitors before who had offered her love, but not the security that she so desperately desired.

She thought of Jesus' soft voice that modulated across the air and seared into your soul, touched the heart with its sincerity while echoing a strange, melodic ring of authority. His voice haunted her. It was as if she had met him somewhere before during her childhood, talked to him on some silent country road, in a crowded city street, in the darkness when afraid. And always in talking with him her spirit had been lifted up so many years ago, and now he had come back into her life. No, his voice had re-entered her consciousness, having risen from the recesses of a mind that had forgotten childhood, had fallen prey to the struggles of every day life.

She thought about what he had said to her earlier in the day. "There are those whose better selves lie slain by their own hand out of desperation. Many people let the worse-self grow too strong; and thereby, it will ever be the master. The person will try to flee from it, but it will follow like the angel of death. Escaping it is difficult. Insult it and it will chastise you with burning shame, with stinging self-reproach from day to day, but you can defeat it by the courage to look at yourself, look deep within and find the tenderness that will let you walk the way of sunlight."

Cap Johnson and his wife also lay in bed. They were not speaking, but they did not have to speak, because the effect Jesus had on them was similar to the effect he had on Virginia. Neither of them could find a reason why, but they turned and looked at each other with knowing glares that simply said, without words, that the man downstairs had, with his simple incantations of wisdom, wrought a profound change within them.

Love and marriage are not always synonymous, but on this night, for these two elderly people, the love that had almost died raised itself from the depths of an ocean of despair and broke through the surface to bask in the bright sunshine of hope. They embraced and sighed in the throes of the realization that the man they just met had breathed life back into their marriage.

Meanwhile, Jesus decided to take a stroll, so he walked out onto the landing of the boarding house, looked about as the fog began to roll in, took in a deep breath of moist night air, turned to his right and began to meander down the street toward First Avenue in search of someone he had noticed looking out the window of the Dunsmuir Club at him. Yes, he was about to reconnect with a man who was as atheistic as anyone could get, but he was a man of deep compassion, and an intrepid devotion to the cause of justice. Jesus had once said to Aaron Adams, "I know far too many devoted Christians who are infected with a disease called hypocrisy, and I also know many atheists like you, who do a much better job of serving God than those who talk the talk but do not walk the walk." Jesus needed help in the task he was about to undertake. The kind of help only a man like Aaron Adams could provide.

Jesus could feel in the darkness behind him the lurking evil that had always pursued him, always tried to erect a barrier to the sanctification of justice for those who toiled daily in obscurity to combat the evil that permeated a world where the many were in complete servitude to the privileged few.

Tolkien had described darkness better than any other writer, and Jesus knew well how he had stated that darkness generally triumphed over the light in a world where those in power embraced darkness rather than the light. Jesus knew, as did Tolkien, that darkness had no beginning, and that neither will it ever have an end. So then, it is eternal and, despite his best efforts, the darkness generally triumphed, which is why he had been crucified in so many ways so many times by those who hypocritically claimed to love him, but served not him, but the forces of darkness. Where the light cannot come, there abides the darkness of men's souls. The light was always being suppressed by evil that hollowed a mine out of the infinite expression of the darkness. Jesus always felt like Tolkien's passing flame, moving quietly amid the surrounding night, was the only hope for mankind, but there were so many who served evil and wanted to extinguish that flame with the putrid breath of hypocrisy.

The world is a dangerous place to live, not because of the people who are evil, but because of the people who do not do anything about that evil, but Jesus and Aaron Adams were two men who never cowered before malicious wickedness. Yet, on this night, Jesus felt trepidation, because he could sense something evil behind him, something that was hiding in the darkness and the fog. Jesus knew that there was always a fine line separating good and evil that passes right through every human heart. This line shifts as inside us it oscillates with the years. And even within hearts overwhelmed by good, there can be a bridgehead of evil; therefore, even in the best of all hearts, there remains a small corner of evil. Jesus knew it was impossible to expel evil from the world in its entirety, but it was possible to constrict it within each person. However, there are people who have no remnants of good whatsoever, and he had the ability to feel palpable evil, and on this night in the dark and fog, there behind him he could sense evil of the foulest kind, an evil that was right there in Ladysmith to do incalculable harm and to wrap the town in a blanket of heinous malevolence.

WHEN JESUS CAME TO LADYSMITH
TO BATTLE THE ANGEL OF DEATH

Jesus had seen the evil of darkness in the streets of many cities before, the kind that makes the street like an old fashioned photograph, everything a shade of grey. The darkness on this night was much worse, as it had no grey tint, only black. It was a darkness that robs you of your best sense and replaces it with a paralysing fear. In this kind of darkness, muscles get cramped and you are unable to move. If it had been any other person but Jesus, or maybe Aaron Adams, the fear might lead to a mad flight from whatever it was that lurked about behind him.

Jesus could hear nothing, as the silence was almost deafening. He had the senses of a predator when battling evil, but in the darkness of this night it was he who was the prey. From the perspective of the person being chased, fear is a natural response but this was not the response of a man with the courage and intense fortitude Jesus possessed. His head and heart went to the riveting place that crushes fear and projects a beam of intense radiance to bring a comforting spark that lights righteousness and elevates fortitude in the battle between good and evil.

He heard the flapping of wings and turned to face whatever it was with the determination of righteousness. The thing was there before him, or was it just a figment of his imagination? Regardless, rather than fearing it, Jesus said with great assurance, "Be gone you devil of despair, vanish from the sight of he who stands against evil."

Was it real or imagined?

Chapter 7
You Always Lose the War

Thou all fear the angel of death
That waits for thee at the portals of the skies
Ready to suck away thy final breath,
Ready with black hand to close thine eyes.

How many a begging soul has passed away,
Fleeing in pain as the light grows dark
To the eternal embrace of the blackest day,
Where the hounds of death brazenly bark.

Spirits too tender for the battle here
Snatched from life, its hopes, its fears, its charms,
And everyone, shuddering at a word so drear,
Has begged for mercy in death's arms.

J. Wayne Frye   139

WHEN JESUS CAME TO LADYSMITH
TO BATTLE THE ANGEL OF DEATH

He whom thou fear will relish your pain,
And lay his cold hand upon thy aching heart,
Will stir the terrors of thy troubled brain,
And bid your stinging soul to depart.

Oh, what was life, if life was at all?
Blinded darkness steals your breath,
As evil embraces your final fall,
For here comes the Angel of Death!

Aaron and Hobbs sat sipping on drinks at a table in front of the window facing First Avenue, where Hobbs had walked that faithful night before turning right and going down another street toward his hotel, the very street where he had wound up in front of a house that he entered and found a body with the heart missing, a body that the police had discovered no trace of.

Hobbs had gulped his drink with gusto, so Aaron waved at the waitress, but she had a tray in her hand and was headed toward another table. The bartender, noticing Aaron's signal, meandered over and said, "Yes, what I may get you two? More drinks?"

"My friend will have another scotch and soda. Nothing more for me," offered Aaron.

The bartender smiled down at Hobbs and said, "Glad to see you calmer than the last time you came in."

WHEN JESUS CAME TO LADYSMITH
TO BATTLE THE ANGEL OF DEATH

Surprised, Hobbs glared at the bartender as Aaron said, "When was it that you saw him?"

"Oh, I see a lot of people. Goes with the job, but I remember him because he came in twice on the same night awhile back. Can't give you the exact date, though. Just remember it because of the strange thing that happened when he came in the second time."

"Strange thing?" asked Aaron.

"Yeah, he looked really frightened."

"You have any idea just how long he was in here?"

"Not long. It was foggy that night. I remember that. He was here just a few minutes. Long enough to guzzle down a drink with shaking hands. He had to hold it with both hands he was so nervous. He kept looking out the window, and then a guy with a dark hood over his head looked in the window. He was sitting right here at this table. The guy motioned to him, and almost like he was hypnotized, he got up and walked out. I saw him from the bar, and I was so intrigued with the man looking in the window that I walked over and went to the door. I looked out in the street, and I noticed that they walked down past High Street, which is the next street and then down to Buller, which is the next street after High."

Aaron said, "And you saw them turn right then?"

"No, they turned left," said the bartender as he walked away.

Wam, bam, shazam! That's the bonus of having low expectations. Expect nothing and people will surpass your expectations with aplomb. High expectations are just a one way ticket to disappointment. Low expectations are the secret ticket to getting what you don't expect. Hobbs turned left, not right, and he turned two streets down not one street down. Things were falling into place.

Shock registered on Hobbs' drawn face. A distinguishable fear played on his trembling lips. It wasn't what he said, because he was too shocked to say anything at first, but he was muttering with unintelligible words that were like tart lemon pudding that makes you pucker but still savour the sourness that invaded your mouth. Finally, some distinguishable words came out. "I, I, I don't understand. I have no recollection of being here a second time, and I am sure I turned right at the next corner. Something doesn't add up."

"Stop and reflect. Think real hard," said Aaron. "The bartender said you looked frightened. What would have frightened you? Come on now. Think real hard."

WHEN JESUS CAME TO LADYSMITH
TO BATTLE THE ANGEL OF DEATH

The bartender placed down Hobbs' drink as he looked out the window and said, "There's another strange one peering in. That one really looks like trouble."

As the bartender walked away and Hobbs was in deep thought, Aaron turned to look out the window and realized the bartender was right in predicting the person peering in represented some real trouble. Oh my, there he was!

There may be better people in the world than Aaron Adams, but there was, without any doubt whatsoever, absolutely no one better at standing, without any fear, against despicable injustice than he and that man calling himself Jesus who was now staring in the window with a crooked smile on his lips. Aaron had seen him walking up the main street of Ladysmith, and knew at the very first glance that where that man went, trouble inevitably followed. Unfortunately, he also was a man who seemed to lure Aaron into the trouble with him.

Aaron had absolutely no fear of the devil, because frankly, he had no religious beliefs within him whatsoever, but he did have a very strong belief in evil, because he dealt with it constantly as part of his profession. Yet, for all his scepticism, he realized that there were unexplainable things that mystified him, made him question his own reason. This man titillated those thoughts and made him question whether or not there really was something almost godly about this person.

Three times before he had encountered Jesus, and each time the man had stirred up elements that lit a raging fire of hatred toward him among those who talked about being Christians, but did nothing to promote the true Christian creed. Like those who demanded the crucifixion of the Biblical Jesus, he had actually seen modern day men turn their backs on someone who epitomized the very nature of love, but the man he knew was also a true revolutionary in the mould of Che Guevara, a man who encouraged people to never bow before the authority of the unjust. Aaron could not help but shudder at the thought of what this supreme rebel with a noble commitment to justice was about to unleash on the town of Ladysmith. The Jesus he knew was someone capable of deep, abiding love. He was also a man the unthinking, the politicians and the religious power structure feared. These people stood in deep dread of him. Yet, they feared him for another simple reason; he questioned the power structure and to those in power that was intolerable. He was a man who never mentioned having supernatural power, never suggested he was the son of God and never said he could perform miracles. Rather, he told ordinary people they had the power to perform miracles, the inexorable power to challenge authority, challenge a world where the many were in economic and social bondage to the few. He promoted rebellion against injustice, just as the Jesus in the Bible did. He believed in the sanctity of the common person and the power of the common person to band with others and demand justice from a corrupt system that enslaved 99% to the 1%. That was an idea that made those in power shiver in fear that people might actually listen to him and make a determined stand against injustice.

Aaron, shaking his head in frustration, took a deep breathe and said to Hobbs "I am sorry, but the man looking in that window is someone who obviously wants to talk with me. Can I ask him in? We'll continue our conversation in a bit."

"Of course," replied Hobbs.

Reluctantly, Aaron motioned for Jesus to come in. He felt deep inside that he might better serve his own sanity by ignoring him, but Jesus was a man you could not ignore. The path of life is challenge enough, without making mountains out of molehills, and yeah, we all see the craggy mountain of ice when we are afraid, triggered, maxed out emotionally and need to climb to the summit and escape the agonies that abide in the valleys below. Jesus was a man who had climbed many mountains, and Aaron had been with him three times on the climbs and was impressed that the ascent never exhausted him. So instead of that high drama that goes with the fatigue of failure in

WHEN JESUS CAME TO LADYSMITH
TO BATTLE THE ANGEL OF DEATH

a world that never really embraces humanity, but rather scorns it in service to the privileged class, Jesus' energy come down to something softer that solidified the realization that a better world was possible, but Aaron, deep inside, knew a better world was impossible as long as the privileged few were in complete control of everything. Those poor souls who could destroy the system of favouritism that had afflicted humanity since its inception were too busy with the burdens of everyday life and bowing before patriotic flag-waving to ever stand against the tyranny that made slaves out of 99% of the population. Aaron saw Jesus as Don Quixote chasing windmills. And what did that make Aaron, who three times now had stood by his side only to see catastrophe ensue? Yeah, Aaron was the modern servant to Don Quixote. He was the frustrated Sancho Panza in service to an insane man who was chasing windmills.

Jesus, with his long flowing hair, somewhat unkempt appearance and determined stride walked into the restaurant. Aaron said to him as he sat down, "I would say I am glad to see you, but I would be lying."

Jesus, smiling, replied "Aaron, when I saw you looking out that window of the exclusive club where the elite of the town prance around like peacocks, I knew that my quest would be aided by he who is a champion of justice, but this time I am not here to rile up the citizenry, but to make a grand stand against evil of the absolute vilest kind, an evil that could destroy this beautiful place."

Jesus looked over at Hobbs and continued, "And you, Mr. Hobbs, I believe have seen that evil up close."

Aaron and Hobbs were most mystified with Jesus' familiarity with Hobbs. Aaron said, "How do you know Hobbs?"

Smiling, Jesus replied, as he reached out to shake Hobbs' hand, "Pleasure to meet you." While shaking hands, Jesus turned to Aaron and said in response to his question about knowing Hobbs, "Why Aaron, I know everything. Am I not the son of man?"

Shaking his head vehemently, Aaron took a deep breath and said to Hobbs, "So now you are acquainted with the terror of tribulations, the man who causes more trouble than a hurricane roaring ashore and actually does more damage."

"Such compliments," interjected Jesus.

"Believe me. I am not complimenting you."

Jesus, ignoring Aaron, looked over at Hobbs and said, "You have encountered unbridled evil have you not?"

Mystified, Hobbs replied, "I don't know, but I know what I saw was the result of evil, yes."

Turning his gaze to Aaron, Jesus said "So, tell me all about Hobbs' problem, because I think it might be related to my problem as well."

Aaron spent the next few minutes going over, with Hobbs' permission, what the two were facing in terms of a mystery they could not figure out. When Aaron finished, Jesus looked over at Hobbs and said, "There are those here, in this beautiful place, who long to summon an evil angel, the angel that is feared by all. It is known as the Angel of Death, and he carries a scythe that must be sharpened with the blood of human hearts, because the fresh heart gives the blade of the scythe power that is conveyed to the angel. The angel walks about the earth during the day as any human would, until the murder of an innocent allows it to manifest itself as the dark evil creature with wings. He was banned from heaven. Samael (sometimes called Samiel, Samsama'il, Samail), is often referred to as the Venom of God, the Poison of God or more appropriately the Angel of Death. Like Satan, he is a fallen angel, a figure who is the accuser, the seducer and the destroyer. He is assigned grim and destructive duties as the angel of death and the head of Satan's minions that want to bring on the Apocalypse in order to enter the final battle for earth with Jesus Christ. He condones the sins of evil men and promotes them

WHEN JESUS CAME TO LADYSMITH
TO BATTLE THE ANGEL OF DEATH

as good. He was banished and cursed by God, and joined the legions of fallen angels who are allied with Satan. To take revenge, he tempts and connives with those who embrace the dark side. It is he who was the real father of Cain, having slipped into Eve's bed of straw while Adam slept to procreate the evil son (Cain) who would slay his own brother. He is also assumed to be the partner of Lilith, who was Adam's first wife. Lilith like Samael, can morph between human form and that of a demon. Together, they relish with great joy the sowing of evil among humans and the promotion of everything that will assist in facilitating the final battle between the good of Jesus and the evil of Satan. However, there is one thing that stands in the way before the battle can begin. It is the Seven Seals."

Aaron, shaking his head and sighing, offered an observation. "Save us all that Biblical crap. Neither of us is a fool. There is no God, and even if there was a God I have no use for a deity that would allow the misery which permeates the earth. What kind of grotesque, perverse God would allow all the suffering that goes on every day? And the absurdity of a saviour named Jesus is beyond the pale. He is but a thought, a vagrant thought, a useless thought, a homeless thought, wandering with promises among fools who are too timid to think for themselves, fools who actually believe that all their suffering will get them a reward in the end in a paradise where they will sit around on a floating cloud all day plucking their harps."

Looking over at Hobbs, Jesus said, "I love this man. He doubts, but yet he honours everything Jesus stands for with his battle against injustice."

Aaron said, "So you are here to find something called the Seven Seals, and we are in search of something almost as elusive, a disappearing house where Mr. Hobbs saw a dead body with the heart removed."

"That is the abject irony of our being in the same place at the same time, Aaron. You see, the Seven Seals are always being sought by the Angel of Death, also called, as I alluded to earlier, Samael. It is absolutely no coincidence, I assure you, that Mr. Hobbs saw a corpse with the heart removed. You see, there is a cult that worships Samael. It is called the Cult of the Seven Seals, because they believe that cutting out the hearts of people with a scythe is a way of appeasing Satan and locating the Seven Seals. They are here in Ladysmith, and that means the Seven Seals are most likely here, too. Unless I recover them first, there will be a great calamity that will engulf this lovely little paradise by the sea, and eventually the whole world."

Hobbs asked, "Just what are these Seven Seals to which you refer?"

WHEN JESUS CAME TO LADYSMITH
TO BATTLE THE ANGEL OF DEATH

Jesus, with great conviction in his voice, replied, "In the Book of Revelation, the Seven Seals are the seven symbolic seals that secure the book that John of Patmos saw in an apocalyptic vision. The opening of the seals of the document occurs in Revelation Chapters 5–8 and marks the Second Coming of Christ and the beginning of the time of great tribulation – the Apocalypse. In John's vision, the only one worthy to open the book/scroll is referred to as both the Lion of Judah and the lamb having seven horns and seven eyes."

While Jesus spun his tale of woe, Aaron shook his head and sighed. It was obvious he believed little of what Jesus was saying. Yet, he knew there was always some substance to anything that this remarkable man had to wisely impart.

"The opening of the Seven Seals will unleash cataclysmic events that will usher in the end of times, but the minions of Satan want to begin the battle before Christ is ready. Thus, their eternal search for the seals, so evil can triumph over good. The Book of Daniel warns against opening the book before the Lamb is ready to ascend his throne. Upon the opening of a seal from the book, a judgment is released or an apocalyptic event occurs. The opening of the first four Seals releases the Four Horsemen, each with his own specific mission. The opening of the fifth Seal releases the cries of martyrs for the wrath of God. The Sixth Seal prompts earthquakes and other cataclysmic

J. Wayne Frye   151

events. The Seventh Seal cues seven grand trumpeters, and after their appearance more cataclysmic events follow. Now, I know my friend Aaron here thinks this is all a grand fantasy of delusional people who are wrapped up in religion, and I never promote belief one way or another, but I do promote the fact that evil abides in the hearts of many who proclaim to be Christians. I have always adhered to the idea you judge a person by their actions rather than by their pronouncements. It is awfully easy to judge someone and point the vile finger of condemnation, and unfortunately, that is what far too many believers do. It is always my aim to point out those who practice hypocrisy."

"And what makes you think this may be related to what I discovered in that house?"

"The body with a missing heart is emblematic of what occurs consistently among the Cult of the Seven Seals. The pattern has been repeated for thousands of years in different places all over the world. They make a human sacrifice to the Angel of Death, so that his scythe can be polished with the blood from a recently removed human heart. The cult is made up of wealthy people whose primary aim is to garner more wealth for themselves through service to Satan's henchmen. They believe that if the Angel of Death can open the Seven Seals before the prescribed time, then they will be exalted and saved from the

Apocalypse. However, the Seven Seals have been kept safe by being constantly moved about by a group that was once known as the Knights Templar. The descendants of the original Knights Templar guard that relic today, and other descendants guard the Holy Grail."

Hobbs said, "I am not very religious. Could you tell me about the knights?"

"The Knights Templar were in charge of preserving the Holy Grail, which is the cup from which Jesus drank at the Last Supper. They were disbanded by the Catholic Church, because they became too powerful, and the church can have no one around that will usurp its power. Of course, they never surrendered the Grail and descendants of the original Knights continue to guard it to this day, although no one knows where it is and who the modern Templars are. It is also rumoured that they discovered the Seven Seals in a cave during the Crusades and have been guarding it since the Middle Ages."

As Jesus discussed the seals and the Holy Grail, Aaron noticed that sitting at the table next to them was a person who seemed to be vehemently interested in what they were discussing as she appeared to be straining to hear. She was maybe 24 or 25 and possessed curves of softness. She was not the model-type with bodies that seemed emaciated. Rather, she had the muscles of a footballer and the blessed fat of a baby; she was astonishingly gorgeous in almost every way. There's beauty in being an astute listener, and the attentive listening she was doing made her beauty profound. Her eyes showed a sorrowfully concerned soul. They were a deep pool of restless brown, a dark ocean of longing for solace and hope. As Aaron looked into her eyes he felt all the beauty of the universe could not even hope to compete with the simple thing that radiated from her and glowed like a bright light in the darkness. Still, she possessed an inner passion that turned those twinkling eyes into orbs of the brightest fire, and in them he read clearly that she would fight to the very last breath for what she believed in. She would not let the world break her or anyone or anything she valued. She had a beauty that made those billboard-princesses and magazine-Barbies look as paper thin and shallow as they are. She was something robust and real, so real that the sixty-three year old Aaron, who had lost most of his libido long ago, sensed a tingle between his legs.

Her eyes were tilted downward in an attempt to feign disinterest in Aaron, but Aaron's stare was recognizable to her without even looking. Then, her eyes tilted upward and met his. She smiled. So beautiful was the smile that it was like the stars themselves decided to rest behind the soft cushion of her thick succulent lips that seemed to be begging for a moist kiss. Aaron sighed, and the astute Jesus, who had been enthralling both the woman and Hobbs with his spellbinding oratory, noticed Aaron, despite his age, was titillated by the woman across from him. Ever the romantic, Jesus said to him, "Why don't you ask the lady to join us?"

Aaron lowered his head and replied, "I am a bit old for her."

"Old is in the mind."

Aaron, smiling and looking downward said, "And also somewhere else."

Smiling, Jesus said, "Nichola, want you join us?"

Aaron and Hobbs were shocked that Jesus would know the woman. In addition, she, herself, reflected shock that he knew her, based upon her confused look. Smiling, Jesus motioned for her to join them.

When she rose from her seat, the whole room slowed down. She had perfect dark hair that rested right above her shoulders and her gait was that of a woman imbued with the supreme confidence that she could command anything of any man and he would grovel before her. She had perfect skin that looked so fragile, and so soft with unerring freckles around her nose that danced with seductiveness in the pale light of the room. Her body moved carefully forward like a warrior readying for battle. Her small waist was hidden under a red ribbed top, and her curvy hips were like hairpin turns on a dangerous raceway. She fit so perfectly in her dark strategically torn blue jeans that it appeared they had been drawn on her lithe body. Aaron rose and pulled out a chair for her to take a seat. As she did, her eyes were trained on Jesus, as she said, "Do I know you?"

With that patented grin, Jesus replied, "No, but I know you."

"Could you explain?"

"No. I cannot."

Confused, she looked over at Aaron. "Maybe you could explain, then?"

"My dear lady, I can explain almost nothing about this man, unfortunately. He is an enigma I have been trying to figure out for years, and when he tells you his name you will be more confused."

Taking a deep breath, which Aaron found titillating as her voluptuous breasts heaved upward, she asked Jesus, "And what is your name?"

"I am called Jesus."

WHEN JESUS CAME TO LADYSMITH
TO BATTLE THE ANGEL OF DEATH

Laughing out loud, Nichola looked over at Hobbs and said, "And you, I suppose, are John the Baptist."

Smiling, Hobbs extended his hand and said, "No, I am not so famous. My name is Calvin Hobbs."

She then looked over at Aaron and said, "You I know, which is why I was staring, because I have been in New York often and occasionally seen your picture in the *New York Times*. Of course, I have also read a few Wayne Frye books detailing your exploits. You are Aaron Adams. I hope you will forgive me for staring."

Aaron was never overly impressed with his press clippings or Wayne Frye's somewhat embellished detailing of his more famous cases. He said, "Believe me, I am often overrated by the press, and definitely overrated by Wayne Frye's lurid novels. As for staring at me, I am flattered such a gorgeous woman would warrant me a commodity worthy of stare."

Sheepishly smiling now, she replied, "Well, I assume his vivid descriptions of your sexual exploits are overrated too, then?"

Laughing out loud, Aaron said "Believe me beautiful lady; those are absolutely the most overrated of all."

WHEN JESUS CAME TO LADYSMITH
TO BATTLE THE ANGEL OF DEATH

With twinkling eyes that were filled with mischievousness, Nichola interjected "Well, I am a woman who has to find things out for myself. I never believe anything without absolute solid proof."

Jesus looked over at Hobbs and said, "Nichola here is a very unusual woman."

"Why do you say that? asked Nichola.

"Because of whom you are named after."

"I am named after my aunt."

"And who was she named after?"

"Oh, I believe it was some famous woman warrior way back in the Middle Ages."

"Actually," said Jesus, "Nichola was a member of an adjunct to the Knights Templar. They were called the Order of the Hatchet. They called the order that, because when the Spanish town of Tortosa was attacked by the Moors, most of the men had departed for the Crusades, and there were only old men, women and children left. The women armed themselves with hatchets and fought the Moors so fiercely that the Moors, although not defeated, were so impressed with the bravery of the women that they stopped the siege and left. When the Knights Templar heard of the bravery of these women, they founded the Order of the Hatchet to honour them and their bravery. Thus, the women became knights, and the fiercest warrior among those knights was the woman called Nichola."

"Interesting," offered Nichola. "You are up on history, but I knew that. I suppose one would say my aunt was a bit of a warrior herself. She was a determined promoter of women's rights, of the rights of the poor and disenfranchised. She believed that silence in the presence of oppression was acquiescing to your own enslavement. She was arrested and jailed often in her fight against injustice. In fact, when she was dying from cancer, she was still attending demonstrations in support of the cause for justice."

Jesus took a deep breath and said as he exhaled, "Standing against injustice is a lonely battle, and most times a fruitless exercise in frustration. People actually, as a result of brainwashing patriotic babble and religious subterfuge, vote against their own best interests. Brainwashed religious and patriotic zealots are easily manipulated by a corrupt system that serves the interests of the privileged class and the evil they embrace that traps the 99% in eternal bondage to the idea they are free, which is an illusionary idea that is promoted to keep people in line. Defy authority and you are locked up as an example to others who might dare question authority."

WHEN JESUS CAME TO LADYSMITH
TO BATTLE THE ANGEL OF DEATH

Aaron, having experienced Jesus' revolutionary rhetoric before, shook his head and said, "You are chasing windmills my friend. Things never change for two reasons. Number one, people are too engrossed watching what the Kardashians are doing or getting excited over a mindless situation comedy that uses canned laughter to remind people to laugh, and number two, people are too complacent after years of watching things never change that they have simply given up in frustration. The money changers are continually let back into the temple. The truth is that evil always triumphs over good." He sighed and continued. "You are proof of that. Everything you have tried to accomplish always ends with evil triumphant in the end. I have seen you win small victories, win a battle here and there, but you always lose the war."

WHEN JESUS CAME TO LADYSMITH
TO BATTLE THE ANGEL OF DEATH

Chapter 8
Among the Forgotten Ones

She is the daughter of the sunny flocks.
She breathes sanctity in the secret air.
Her beauty never fades from the mortal day.
In the darkness her soft voice is heard,
And her gentle lamentation falls like morning dew.

Oh life, she is the lotus of the water?
She is the child of the emerging spring?
She is the reflection in a crystal glass.
She is the soft shadow in the water.
She is like the dreams of infants,
Like a smile upon a baby's face,
Like the dove's voice, like transient day,
Like music in the air; she is natures finest.

J. Wayne Frye   161

WHEN JESUS CAME TO LADYSMITH
TO BATTLE THE ANGEL OF DEATH

She is the sunshine through dark clouds,
The lily of the valley breathing in the humble grass,
The willowy sunflower swaying gently in the breeze,
The gilded butterfly that perches on a limb.
She is the morning glory that smiles on all.

She walks in the valley each morn with soft steps
Saying, "rejoice thou humble grass,
Thou sweet new-born lily flower,
Thou gentle silent valleys and modest brooks;
For thou shalt be clothed in light,
And fed with grand morning manna,
Till summers heat melts willingly
Beside the fountains and the springs
That flourish in your glory and reach for the sun.

This is the demon hunter of great renown,
Whose grandeur and glory everywhere is found.
Her name rolls over the tongue like warm honey.
When saying it, all turn to whisper,
As it makes the name seem crisper.
As honest as that man named Lincoln;
Say her name, say her name: Lynton!

Hobbs felt his predicament had been lost in the conversation which had floated into esoteric philosophy rather than the precarious state in which he found himself. It was then that Aaron, noticing his consternation, said, "Believe it or not, your plight is actually tied into what we are discussing. You see, there is, I believe, some type of evil plot afoot here in Ladysmith."

WHEN JESUS CAME TO LADYSMITH
TO BATTLE THE ANGEL OF DEATH

Hobbs, delighted that his predicament was now back as the focal point of the conversation said, "So, you are saying that the mission of Jesus here in search of the Seven Seals is tied up with my seeing that dead body?"

Jesus, interrupting Aaron just as he was about to speak, said "It is, because you see what you described is part of the aforementioned ritual to summon the Angel of Death who requires the sharpening of his scythe blade with fresh blood from a human heart. The angel, whether real or imagined, is here in search of the Seven Seals. Now, is it a real evil angel, or is it simply someone dressing up and trying to convince people he is the Angel of Death. I am not much of a believer in the supernatural, but I do believe in evil, and those who want to serve the cause of evil. I look at the culture of greed, and know that evil is embraced by more than a handful of capitalists. Evil is allowed to flourish, because good men and women refuse to confront it. Those who do not embrace it, but turn a blind eye to it are also guilty."

Aaron said, "We need to go down the street two blocks, turn left and see if you can recognize anything."

As Aaron was speaking, someone extraordinary walked in, a person who was, like Aaron, famous for her detecting skills, as well as her well-documented acumen in regards to demon hunting.

WHEN JESUS CAME TO LADYSMITH
TO BATTLE THE ANGEL OF DEATH

This striking Filipino-Canadian woman's beauty could not be understated; perhaps it was because she disarmingly disregarded her own haunting attractiveness. Her dark skin was not completely flawless, but her manner made one disregard any flaw as nothing more than a complimentary pattern that elevated her beauty. It is doubtful that she ever once used face masks or expensive beauty products. That really wasn't her modus operandi. She was all about simplicity, making things easy, helping those around her to relax and be happy in a world she saw as placing a burden on the many for the pleasure of the few. Perhaps that is why, despite her intense concern for the downtrodden and forgotten, her skin still glowed like a rain-burnished rose under the emerging sun after a summer downpour. It was her inner beauty that lit her eyes like periods on a billboard at the end of a sentence and softened her features to reflect the depth of her kindness, but there was also a determination that was present in every confident stride she took, seeming to say, "I am not a woman with whom you want to trifle." Oh, and her thick succulent lips that were usually slightly parted seemed ready for a wet passionate kiss, making most men, and probably even some women, pulsate with carnal desires. And her mischievous smile was one of happiness growing much as a spring flower opens. You could see how it came from deep inside to light her eyes and spread into every part of her meticulous perfectly proportioned body. It was a soft, sincere smile that

J. Wayne Frye

glowed like the sun had toppled down from the sky and made a home in her heart. If there was a God, this was his masterpiece; his pièce de résistance!

Her emotions were not easily hidden on her innocent face. Her concern was evident in the crease of her lovely brow and the down-curve of her full lips. But her eyes showed her soul. They were a deep pool of restless black. Passion turned her eyes into orbs of the brightest fire, and in them one could read clearly that she was a fighter against evil. She would not let the world break people, especially her. With black hair flowing down to her waist fluttering with each stride, she held her head high and waltzed on with an effortless saunter. The clicking of her heels added rhythm to the soft classical music that played onward without pause. Her eyes scanned the room with determination in search of someone, and when her eyes met Aaron's she smiled. So beautiful was the smile that it was like the stars decided to rest behind the soft cushion of her lips. She could have graced any billboard or magazine cover, but she was better than those two dimensional photo-shopped models. Somehow her imperfections made her perfect. There was no implied shyness to her, no hesitation in her determined body movements, and when she spoke directly to Aaron Adams there was softness in her voice as she almost whispered through those pouty, puckered, thick lips. "Hello there."

WHEN JESUS CAME TO LADYSMITH
TO BATTLE THE ANGEL OF DEATH

Her white suit had a tailored look that was bold against her dark skin, but everyone at the table imagined her as more comfortable in jeans and a t-shirt. She was right there, less than a foot away, but in her understated glamour she might as well have been on the television, on a movie screen or in a music video.

Aaron stood up, smiled and could see in her demeanour why her husband, Wayne Frye, always called her his little headache. Wherever she went she caused chaos among both men and women who were mesmerized by her plucky attitude and incredible depth of personal magnetism. Aaron pulled out his chair and signalled for her to take a seat, as he said, "this little lady is the famous demon hunter, Lynton Viñas Frye."

Each person introduced themselves as she gracefully acknowledged them, and then turned to Aaron to say, "You called me to ask if you could stay at my home, but I instinctively knew that there was a storm of controversy brewing. I could sense it in your voice, and you know I simply cannot resist a mystery. Wayne is back east on a book tour to promote his latest novel, and he told me to let you stay, but to not get involved in any of your shenanigans." Then she looked at Jesus and continued, "Now, with Jesus here, I am really going to get into trouble, because Wayne once said the two of you together were like TNT with a short fuse."

WHEN JESUS CAME TO LADYSMITH
TO BATTLE THE ANGEL OF DEATH

Beauty, the attribute of heaven,
Is in various forms to mortals given.
No hand spun lace was ever so fine,
As Lynton's beauty penetrated the mind.

Search the wide world, go where you will,
This is a woman divine and never still.
Capricious nature knows no bound,
'Cause women like her are rarely found.

In every movement, she displays grace,
With a knowing smile on her face.
Women like her could drown oceans,
Sitting waves in constant motion.

Wayne telling Lynton to stay out of trouble was like telling a fish to stay out of water. This was a woman who never wavered when confronted with evil, and when Aaron and Calvin related the story, she eagerly said she would help solve the mystery, and then she turned to Jesus and said, "You believe that somehow the Seven Seals are connected to this don't you?"

"Definitely," replied Jesus.

"Let's get started," said Lynton.

It was like an army of the determined as Lynton, Aaron, Jesus, Hobbs and Nichola walked at a brisk pace, as if they were headed for a rendezvous with destiny. Actually, they were!

J. Wayne Frye   167

WHEN JESUS CAME TO LADYSMITH
TO BATTLE THE ANGEL OF DEATH

They stopped at Buller Street and turned left, slowly walking up the hill, waiting for Hobbs to recognize the house he had apparently been in on that faithful night. About four houses up on the right, he came to an abrupt stop and just stood and stared. It was obvious that was the house. It was also obvious that the house had not been lived in for many years.

It was now getting darker, as it was nearing eight o'clock, so they all were motionless in the fading light just waiting for Hobbs to say something. He did not. He just stood staring at the windows that were caked in grime and for the most part boarded up, leaving only the slimmest of slithers for the rays of light to pierce through the small cracks into the house. Despite the fact that he had originally seen the house in dense fog, and this was a clear evening, he knew, without a doubt, this was the place.

Ever the brave one, Lynton said "Come, let's see if we can get inside."

The door was bolted, but Aaron, looking over at the house next door excused himself and walked over and knocked on the door. An elderly lady answered the knock and Aaron asked if she knew the owner of the house next door. She said, "I know the owner, and a damnable man he is. Believe me; you do not want to incur his wrath. He'll have security here before you bat an eye. His

J. Wayne Frye

name is Samael Azazel and he comes by here on occasion. In fact, he was here a few nights ago, and they apparently had a party over there. Don't know what kind of party you'd want to have in that disgustingly dilapidated place, but there were some weird looking characters going in and out, very weird."

Aaron said, "Weird in what way?"

"Well, they all were dressed strange. It was a hot night for this time of year, which made it unusual that they all had on black hoods."

"Black hoods?" asked Aaron.

"Yeah, black hoods pulled over their faces like they didn't want anyone to see them. Now, it was pretty foggy that night, but I got good eyes, really good. Anyway, there was a bright stream of light coming from the house that shined right on the porch at the front door that made things more easily visible. Hey, I admit it. I am a nosey neighbour, and I keep an eye on that place, because you can just sense that there is something not right about that house, something that gives you the shivers."

"So, everyone had hoods you say."

"Yes, everyone," and then she got a puzzled look on her face as she continued, "everyone but one person, one person who came up with another hooded man all by himself."

He asked her if she would step out and look at the man (Hobbs) on the far side of the porch of the house, which she enthusiastically did. As she looked at him, Aaron said "Any chance the one with no hood on looked like that man?"

"Well, can't say for sure about the face, as it was too foggy even for my keen eyes, but he sure has the same profile, same silhouette, same height and same weight from what I can see. Yeah, could be that guy for sure."

"Ma'am, we are trying to solve a bit of a mystery. If you saw us get into that place would you notify the cops? We would really like to nose around a bit. I assure you we are not up to anything nefarious."

"If you can get in, go ahead. And if you happen to drop a match and it burns down all the better. A burned out place would be better than that eyesore there now."

Aaron nodded his head and smiled. He said, "Thank you ma'am. I assure you we won't be dropping any matches."

She smiled back at Aaron and while shaking her head said, "Damn! Too bad."

WHEN JESUS CAME TO LADYSMITH
TO BATTLE THE ANGEL OF DEATH

Aaron walked back over and offered a sobering judgment to his cohorts. "I am going in, and we could be arrested. Anybody want to call it a night, be my guest."

All there, from the looks on their faces, were as determined as he was. Lynton said, "Nobody's calling the cops, because whoever owns this house does not want them here anymore than he wants us here. There was something nefarious that occurred in this place."

As always, with Lynton, you got a woman who could quickly assess any situation and provide a cogent analysis. She turned to Aaron and said, "There comes a time when breaking the law is the morally right thing to do. I believe this to be one of those times."

Aaron told the others to stay out front and wait for him to open the door from inside. He walked around to the back where there was a pathway to a gate on an old dilapidated fence. He walked to the gate, gently swung it open and saw it led to an alley, where a dirt road was well-packed down, indicating that the area residents used it often. Turning back toward the house, holding his cell-phone light on the path, he could see that it had been used recently based upon the flattened remnants of grass. The back way was both entrance and exit most of the time, obviously. He eased up onto the back porch and pushed on the door. It was locked, but the ancient lock was easily pried open with his pocket knife. As he held his light on the room, he realized he was in the kitchen. Time had performed irreversible deeds upon the once proud and mighty home. Walls had eroded away, washing the colours into an amalgamation of drab.

He saw a light switch and quickly turned it on, and just as quickly turned it off. Yes, the electricity was on, so seeing light coming from the place confirmed Hobbs' description. However, for now, Aaron discerned it better to be bathed in darkness than to be drowned in police. He moved his way into the hallway, which was exactly as Hobbs had described it, even down to the bench where the man had been sitting. Great chandeliers and tables lay stagnant. Yet, they held the weight of recent activity. The floors lay expectant, creaking as Aaron moved toward the front door.

Aaron unlatched the front door, and he whispered out of recognition that the walls of the house might be listening, "Come in, and do not turn on any lights. Use your cell-phone lights."

The spirit of the house had rescued itself by sleeping for many years, by retreating into the wood away from the dust and obvious evil which lurked about. The spirit of the house stayed there with the memories of its birth, of the hugs and laughter that once were its colours and music, hoping that one day the gayety might emerge again from the obvious evil that had captured the home.

Lynton, the renowned demon hunter, stood silent looking all about, taking in her surroundings as if the house was speaking to her, whispering things only someone with her acute awareness could comprehend. She scanned the rooms through doorways as she gracefully glided down the hallway, realizing that though the floors were bare and the paint was in need of loving care, though the furniture lay still without the warmth of a family, it stood all the same beneath the flakes and dirt seeming to long for respite from some evil that visited in the darkest nights in search of victims. One of those victims was the house itself. The house had fallen prey to evil.

The other four stood in awe as she silently moved about, touching the walls with hands sliding over them as if searching for the breath of those long gone, searching for the heart beats of those longing for escape, searching for reasons why such ill fortune had befallen the house. She knew that history echoed within the walls. Somewhere within, something or somebody was seething with the pain or was the seething with actual evil itself.

She stood by the dining room entrance and turned to look up the stairs where Hobbs had seen the horrible abomination. The stairwell emanated stagnation. As Lynton moved to the bottom of the stairs, looking up, she shivered at the evil from the top of those stairs, an unbridled evil that craved to commit unspeakable acts of terror. Then, as she touched the wall at the bottom of the stairs, the house seemed to shake, and every door slammed shut. This was a house living under constant shadow, a shadow so dark and perverse that it was as if the devil, himself, had setup residence.

Finally, Aaron broke the deathly silence. "Your interpretation, Lynton?"

She, ignoring Aaron, turned to Hobbs. "You were hypnotized."

Shocked, Hobbs replied, "What?"

"You were given a post-hypnotic suggestion to go to Jack's, wait and then leave with someone, leave and come here. The reason you only have memories of being alone and winding up in the house is part of the post-hypnotic suggestion. You are meant to obliterate from your mind the person who accompanied you. You were sent here for a reason. What reason I do not know?"

Nichola, who had been mostly quiet, offered her interpretation. "It would seem that Mr. Hobbs was a pawn of some type. He was part of a pattern, a pattern that was part of ceremony that was performed right here."

Jesus, taking a seat on the bench and apparently in deep thought stared up over his shoulder at the top of the stairs. He stood, walked up the stairs without a word and when he reached the top landing turned and looked back down at Hobbs. Then, he looked at the floor and then back down at Hobbs again. "This was where you saw the thing, the thing with flapping wings. Am I right?"

"You are right, yes."

"You were gazing at the Angel of Death. This house is where a ceremony of attribution was performed. There was a sacrifice made here, so that the Angel of Death could be exalted and his scythe's blade polished with blood from a human heart. This ceremony prepared his scythe blade for a murder of an innocent, a murder that would eventually help reveal to him the location of the Seven Seals."

Jesus, with consternation, said, "The Knights Templar, or perhaps the Order of the Hatchet, or both are here to protect the seals from the Angel of Death and his minions, but my guess is that like me, and the Angel of Death, they do not know where the Seven Seals are. There is a race between the forces of good and the forces of evil. The force for good wants to locate those seals and secure them before the evil ones unleash them before the son of man is destined to save mankind."

Lynton, astutely listening to Jesus, offered her own observational analysis based upon past experience ferreting out demons all over the world. "Demons are fallen angels and they have intellect and will which have no limits on evil. They become present where we least expect them. In our hearts, the demons find unrepentant sin, fear and unresolved trauma. These demons work to increase the darkness and confine us in it. They seek a place of rest inside us, a home where they belong, because we often embrace the dark side. Being spirits, they do not take up space within us; they become attached to the evil in our hearts. They become present within us, intermingled with our selfishness. Their presence becomes familiar and is part of the scenery of our lives. Evil is an eternal winner in the battle for souls, because we let self-interest isolate us from good. Also, there are places where evil pulsates so prominently you can feel it, almost reach out and touch it. As I stand here in this place I can feel that evil here, feel it in every fibre of this house that is not a home. Rather, it is a den of evil where abominable transgressions have occurred in service to evil."

Nichola said, "I can feel the evil here, too. I am young yes, but old enough to know the depth of evil people are capable of." She then looked over at Aaron and said, "I am glad you are here, because you have made a career out of fighting evil, as has Lynton and Jesus I am sure. I am privileged to be here with all of you."

It was obvious to everyone there, except maybe Aaron, that this young woman was developing a strong attraction to Aaron. Perhaps he was unaware of it simply because he assumed their age difference could never sustain an attraction between them. Yet, he felt that which had long ago departed his life, passion for a woman. He looked at her alluringly thick puckered lips and wondered what it would be like to press his lips against hers, close his eyes and melt into that never-never land of passion in each others arms. Snapping back to reality, he said to Hobbs; "Go over your movements here exactly as they occurred." He then looked over at Nichola who was the only one wearing a watch and told her to time his movements.

Hobbs walked through what he had done, and finally, as he stood by the sofa he looked down and said, "There, there on the sofa," as he pointed at the seat cushion. It was a minuscule spot about the size of a pin head, but the cell-phone light caught its slight glimmer against the blue cushion. It was a red blood spot.

Aaron checked it out, but told Hobbs to ignore it and walk through what else he had done that night, so that he could be timed accurately by Nichola with no interruptions. He did so, and then took a seat on the very bench where the servant had been, as he pointed to the door indicating when he left. He took a deep breath and sighed.

Nichola said, "The whole time is only ten minutes."

Aaron said, "So, you are definitely missing one hour. Something happened in that one hour that you are repressing, something that was, no doubt, so horrid you do not want to face it. My guess is that you were hypnotized, which explains your loss of that time and your fantasizing about the house disappearing. That was a post-hypnotic suggestion to make you forget what actually occurred and where it occurred."

"But how was I hypnotized?" asked Hobbs.

"That is a good question, but one it may be difficult to find an answer to. How many people were you around immediately prior to the incident?" asked Aaron.

"Several people at the club, and I met a few people where Commodore Ray was staying, and of course, Commodore Ray, himself."

Jesus interjected, "Since I am staying at the same place as Commodore Ray, I can attest to the fact that many of those living there seem nefarious even at their best. In fact, the commodore is a person I have questions about. He seems a bit mysterious, and, although I realize he is your friend Mr. Hobbs, I must say the he does not strike me as someone with a stellar character."

"Oh," offered Hobbs, "I would not say he was a great friend, perhaps more a close acquaintance."

As Aaron was talking, Lynton wandered, along with Nichola, back into the area by the sofa. She walked in circles and then back out to the dining room area where she noticed that the floor showed some scratches indicating the table had been moved recently. The four legs sat on what was an obviously expensive and out-of-place rug.

Aaron walked in with the others and said, "You noticed the scratches on the floor indicating it had been moved back to the wall, right?"

"And I thought you had missed it," replied Lynton.

Smiling, Aaron said "I'm' a trained detective. I rarely miss anything that obvious."

"Thank we should see what is under that rug?" asked Lynton.

"What do you think?" replied Aaron as he pushed the table to the wall.

WHEN JESUS CAME TO LADYSMITH
TO BATTLE THE ANGEL OF DEATH

Lynton and Nicola started to roll up the rug and all there stood in awe of what was below it on the floor. Some knew what it was, and others just knew it represented evil.

Jesus turned to Hobbs and said, "You have been, in my opinion, perhaps without even knowing it, part of a satanic ritual. This house has been used

WHEN JESUS CAME TO LADYSMITH
TO BATTLE THE ANGEL OF DEATH

for abominable acts in service to the horned servant of the devil called Baphomet, Samael or as he is often called – the Angel of Death."

Lynton looked directly at Jesus and said, "You are here for the Seven Seals, because the Angel of Death, whether he is perceived or real, has come here also in search of them. That avitarus on the floor indicates that a satanic ritual was performed by a coven that will commit any heinous act to find the seals and unleash what they assume will be havoc on the unsuspecting masses. The seals may be nothing more than a figment of vivid imaginations, but those who want to do evil will use them to call out the real demons of commerce, of false religion, of brutality who will lay waste in the name of Satan. This is a battle between good and evil. That much I do believe. I honour you, sir, but giving yourself a holy name does not make you holy. Anyway, like my friend Aaron, I long ago, as a child, gave up a belief in fairy tales. I do not believe in some magical kingdom up in the sky, but I do believe in hell, a hell most people live every day in the eternal battle against the greed that only rewards those at the top of the economic ladder, while the rest of us must be in an eternal struggle for sustenance, shelter and bare necessities. Furthermore," she said as she turned to Hobbs, "you have apparently been an unwitting participant in what the people who were here believe is a way of satisfying the Angel of Death's insatiable appetite for evil and for locating that which will give him the power to usher in what is the final calamity that will allow a fight for the soul of mankind, a fight between the evil of Samael and the goodness of a man called Jesus."

Nichola stood silent, but reached over and took Aaron's hand. In all this turmoil she had found someone she had wanted all her life, someone she felt a great kinship with, someone who lit a fire of affection in her soul. Aaron felt something that he thought he had lost, but the truth is none of us ever lose our desire to love and be loved. Their age difference melted into the oblivion of true affection.

Of course, there also stood Hobbs, bewildered and thoroughly confused about what had happened to him. Had he participated unwittingly in a satanic ritual? Had he perhaps had a hand in the murder of an innocent? He said to Aaron, "Should we not notify the police of what we have discovered, anonymously, of course, in order to avoid prosecution for trespassing?"

"What have we discovered," replied Aaron, "other than a house where there is a satanic drawing on the floor and a drop of blood on a sofa cushion. Other than that, all we have is your tale of seeing what appeared to be an evil entity at the top of the stairs. With no body and not even proof you were ever in the house, we have nothing solid to offer. Notifying the police at this point would be an exercise in futility. Believe me, in far too many cases, the police are a hindrance to justice rather than a help. Tomorrow, Lynton and I will begin research on this Samael Azazel and see where that may lead us."

Lynton interjected, "I am afraid that if this Azazel is affluent, as he may well be, we may find the police more interested in arresting us for trespassing than finding a killer of someone whose body is nowhere to be found. My experience over the years has led me to surmise that when the wealthy are involved, the first duty of the police is to protect them at all costs. Protecting the wealthy is what police and politicians do."

Aaron said, "Yes, let us all get a good night's rest and we will start fresh in the morning. Things always seem clearer after a good night's sleep."

They replaced the rug and the table, making sure to leave the house exactly as they found it. Quietly leaving by the front door, Hobbs, dejected and concerned, headed back to his hotel.

When the others got back to Jack's, they lingered in front of the place for awhile until Lynton asked Jesus if he would like to go home with her and Aaron. He declined, saying he was very comfortable at the boarding house and had a kinship with a couple of the people there already. Smiling as he left and looking back over his shoulder at Aaron and Nichola, he said, "I think Aaron will not be going home with you either."

Lynton said to Aaron, "Come, we'll walk back to my car."

Nichola took his hand and said, "You are welcome to stay at my place. It is right near here."

Lynton, always ready to promote romance, especially when it involved her old friend Aaron, said with a smile, "Guess I'll go home alone. You two have a good night."

Aaron and Nichola stood there just staring at one another. Aaron was astounded at the feelings he had, feelings that had been resurrected by a woman whom he thought was way too young for him, but you cannot judge the karma of love with anything but the heart. All other forms of measurement are meaningless.

As they stood there under the streetlamp, Nichola traced his masculine lips lightly in her mind. She had the overwhelming urge to kiss him, have him wrap her in his arms and listen to his gentle breathing, watching his eyes ripple like water from skipping stones in a cool stream. She knew that his eager mouth would devour hers, and she would be swept away in the ecstasy of the moment. She gazed into his questioning eyes that were pleading, begging to know what she was thinking. She was about to tell him with a depth of passion that brought a tidal wave of lust from deep inside her. She reached up and put her arms around his neck, pulling herself to his eager mouth. Their lips met and the whole world lit up with the fireworks of passion.

Lynton was walking back to her car when she suddenly got that feeling she got far too often. Someone was following her. No, she was not being followed; she was being chased, chased with a fury.

She always looked heroic and in command of any situation, but not this time, because she knew whatever was following her was in a chase, a chase to render her impotent or even worse, dead. Her face was flushed red and her expression was not of pure panic but close to it. The street was deserted and all she had was her swiftness, guile and determination. Her heart pounded, sending blood to her muscular legs as they readied for a mad dash, but a dash to where. She looked to her right and made an immediate turn. She sprang like a cobra to vault a fence in one smooth, swift move, using her hand on the top of the fence to brace herself as her shapely, muscular legs vaulted hurriedly over the barrier. Her breath came in small spurts, hot and nervous. At her sides, dark fingers curled into sweaty fists, swinging forward as if it would make her faster. Throwing herself forward with even greater abandon, her lungs were pulsating furiously as she desperately sucked in air, but the air didn't seem to be enough as she sprinted forward, never taking time to look back and see who or what was after her. Behind her, she could not hear footsteps, but she was sure she heard the flapping of wings. Regardless, she could not look back? Why she wondered? Then she thought of that old Satchel Page quote, "Never look back, something might be gaining on you."

She found herself on a precipice, looking down at a wired fenced area. She was on a narrow ledge of a concrete barrier that held the dirt back from the field where the fence was. The ledge was as wide as a single foot and with all the grip of black ice. It went right around toward a fenced field. Behind the circular fence was some type of encampment. Most certainly the ledge was never designed to be walked on, let alone run on.

She could almost hear a whisper behind her from whatever it was, "I will hunt you down like the vermin you are and exterminate you. Don't think you can evade me forever; you are already in my cross hairs. I have a violent death waiting for you. So run, run as far as you want, hide in whatever recess of the area you want to occupy, but know that I will find you. You cannot escape me. I promise you not only death, but a painful end beyond measure. Should you ever stop running I will only catch you all the sooner so don't even think about asking for mercy, because I never learned the meaning of the word. I am enjoying meditating on your destruction and the cold leap of joy I will feel when your light is extinguished from this vile planet of mindlessly dumb creatures too stupid to realize they are nothing but fodder in the machinery of evil. That which I cannot exploit in my insane pursuit of evil I will destroy. Is your heart pounding yet? Are your feet burning as they run over the hot coals of evil that society scatters to make all the peasants shiver before the powerful?"

The chase, apparently she surmised, seemed sport for her pursuer. Taking Lynton's life was just a small part of a wider game. She, with her indomitable spirit, thought about turning to face the thing on her trail, but she was smart enough to know that there was a time and place to face your enemy, a time that should be of your own choosing in order to maximize the element of surprise and elevate the chance of victory. However, she knew that victory is rarely assured in a world built on lies to bring hope to the hopeless in dark caves granted the illusion of light. That is the illusion of a world made for the few at the expense of the many. Let people see a faint light in the distance as they struggle to reach it, to desperately crawl out of darkness only to realize the light has been extinguished and now there is another in the far distance that will require more sacrifice and more effort to escape that infernal darkness.

WHEN JESUS CAME TO LADYSMITH
TO BATTLE THE ANGEL OF DEATH

There is no spark of hope, there is no rescue coming, it's just you against evil at every turn, whether it is the evil of exploitation or the evil of a pursuer who is hell-bent on your death. So run for now Lynton and scurry to save your own skin, so you can fight another day. In the current situation you are less than a cold rain drop on a scorching desert. What you bring will evaporate into the sky, leaving the landscape unchanged, barren and desolate, a playground for the evil that is pursuing you.

She moved toward another fence in the distance that had been covered with thin meshed tarp, and she could see a campfire burning within the confines of an encampment right near the highway. From the perspective of the chaser, it was evident that he enjoyed the fear emanating from the person being chased. But in this case, this embodiment of evil intentions could sense the person he was pursuing lacked any real fear, because she was too determined and wily in her determination to escape his wrath. For in this need to escape, her head and heart went to the place that is filled with the light of the will to survive. Her feet slipped outwards on the wet autumn leaves as she rounded a corner, heading toward the encampment with the evening air shocking her throat and lungs as she inhaled deeper and faster. With each footfall, a jarring pain shoot through from ankle to knee. Her heart beat frantically, but fear never crossed her mind, because she was too

J. Wayne Frye

committed to survival to let fear temper her determination.

She swept around to the rear of the encampment, finding the entrance. She bolted inside the encampment and saw twelve yurt huts and came upon a group of people sitting on the ground listening to someone she recognized.

There was Jesus conversing with the twelve homeless people who existed in a city that cared enough to erect twelve yurts for them in a vacant lot. Only a small number of people were homeless, but even a small number was intolerable in a nation that reached out with the hand of compassion. She was safe. She looked up in the sky and a giant bat-like creature with huge flapping wings soared overhead, making its way toward the harbour. She was safe for now.

She stood gazing up at the sky with a sense of relief. Stars filled the sky like pale corn that had been turned into freshly turned ground fodder. It was the promise of life in the darkness, a sense of warmth springing from the terrible ordeal she had just survived. That sky with twinkling stars was a vastness bringing humbleness and an eternal space of gratitude for the cosiness of home in this newfound sanctuary.

Jesus said as he paced around the circle of people there, "Here is my dear friend Lynton. She is a bright light of hope in a world of misery. She is the smile that lights up the darkness. She has seen the face of evil and knows it must be confronted, must be pulled screaming from the dark pit into the light. She is the famous demon hunter, who comes ready for battle, unafraid and with grand determination in a war that has gone on since the beginning of time, the eternal struggle between good and evil." He motioned for her to take a seat in the circle, and she eased down among the forgotten ones.

Chapter 9
You Got That Right

Lynton Viñas is living proof
That you can walk through hell
But still stand before
The devil proud and unbowed.

She is a woman
Who never relies on
Someone else's sword,
Because she carries her own.

She says to doubters, "I am she
Who waits patiently through the night.
I stand defiant before you as one
Who equals the strength of the light."

J. Wayne Frye   191

WHEN JESUS CAME TO LADYSMITH
TO BATTLE THE ANGEL OF DEATH

Listening to Jesus talk with the homeless filled Lynton's heart with respect for someone who had more than the gift of oratory, but projected a sincerity that made her actually ask herself if this man was, indeed, some type of mystic phenomena. If there was such a thing as holy, this man was it.

She had seen too much suffering in her life, both personally and externally, to accept any religious beliefs, but there was something about this man that touched the heart, touched that deep space within human beings that longed to find meaning to life in a world where the brutality of most people's existence begged the question of purpose.

She sat there among the homeless, who were looked upon as the dregs of society, and was spellbound by a man who represented the depth of compassion for those who were victims of the most evil economic system ever invented. There was nowhere in the world where greed was not promoted by governments as a means of lifting people out of poverty, when, in fact, it was the very capitalistic system that fed off poverty, using it to imprison people to the privileged class. No matter the "ism," be it capitalism, communism or socialism, the masses were expected to serve the interests of the privileged class – those who sat on their thrones of excess to garner all the good for themselves at he expense of those who struggled day in and day out for a piece of a dream that did not really exist.

J. Wayne Frye

WHEN JESUS CAME TO LADYSMITH
TO BATTLE THE ANGEL OF DEATH

The pain of poverty had shaped Lynton into a warrior. She had risen from the ashes with a tenacity that bordered on the fanatical. Some would call her stubborn, but the truth was she simply was a determined survivor.

She was living proof of what Kipling said about those who never waver before adversity. She was one who could trust herself when others doubted her. She was one who could wait and not be tired by waiting. She was one who could be lied about but did, herself, not deal in lies. She was one who could be hated, but not give way to hating. She was beautiful of body, but knew her spirit was what she wanted others to judge her by, for she understood beauty was a fleeting thing. She comprehended that triumph and disaster were companions in life, and she had suffered both and was better for it.

She could hear the gossip of knaves that was nothing but a trap for fools. She could be weighted down by misery, but rise up from darkness and burst forth into the bright sunshine of hope. She could watch her hard work be broken into shambles but humbly stoop and build again with worn-out tools and a spirit that might be bent but never broken. She would hold on when others would let go. Sometimes she had little left except the will which says to all who might doubt her, "watch me hold on and never submit to the despair, for I am woman, and I am strong."

WHEN JESUS CAME TO LADYSMITH
TO BATTLE THE ANGEL OF DEATH

Watching the people there clinging desperately to every word rolling off Jesus' silver tongue, she realized he was not a dealer in religion, but a dealer in words; and words are the most powerful drug used by mankind. Words are, of course, a drug that the privileged class wants to control, because words can stir the un-stirrable and rouse the un-rouseable. Throughout history, those with the power to use words have been deemed a threat, and often eliminated. Jesus, Che, Ghandi, King, etc. could not be allowed to stir up the poor with words, because there are more poor than rich, and woe be the day peasants with pitchforks in hand might climb the fences and rampage into the gated estates of those who live in splendorous excess from wealth gained on the backs of the masses.

Lynton took a deep breath and wondered how these twelve people wound up homeless. They were fortunate to live in a nation with compassion, which explained their shelter offered by a magnanimous community that did not want to stigmatize, but rather legitimize their intrinsic worth as human beings. She was so happy to be a Canadian. Her husband, fed up with the culture of greed in the USA, had fortunately immigrated to Canada many years ago. Like him, she understood the corporate capitalism that was exported by America sought to enslave all humanity to the bottom line. She could never understand the acquiescence of Americans through patriotic babble and religion to their own enslavement.

J. Wayne Frye

WHEN JESUS CAME TO LADYSMITH
TO BATTLE THE ANGEL OF DEATH

Jesus looked skyward and said, "There is no sin so great as ignorance. Ignorance is what those in power want for you, because ignorance is a prison that incarcerates your mind."

Lynton understood what Wayne had written about in his three books dealing with Jesus' adventures with Aaron Adams. He was a man who presented a danger to authority, because he had no fear of authority and refused to submit to the ignorance of any controlling entity.

Jesus' spellbinding oratory had her enthralled. He walked about exhorting those before him to not give in to despair. "When lips have drunk deep of the bitter waters of hate, suspicion and despair, all the love in the world will not wholly take away that knowledge which embraced hatred to exalt the rich and powerful over the poor and un-powerful. You, my friends, carry your own matches of disgust with things that keep you imprisoned in a world you did not make. You must band together and strike those matches to light your oppressor's own hell with the raging fires of indignation. Stand up against the tyranny of the ruling class."

With that final thought, Jesus reached down with his hand to lift Lynton from her seat on a log. She rose with admiration glowing in her eyes and said, "You are everything Wayne wrote about you. I am honoured to have finally met you."

WHEN JESUS CAME TO LADYSMITH
TO BATTLE THE ANGEL OF DEATH

"The honour is all mine, Lynton, because you are everything that I have heard about you. Come, and I will walk you to your car. You should be home and in bed this late."

"Well, I should be home, but I have been chased tonight, and I am lucky I wound up here."

Looking up at the sky, Jesus said as they strolled out of the encampment, "You have been chased by unmitigated evil. The Angel of Death is a determined adversary, and he has come here to find the Seven Seals, because he wants to sew mayhem not just in this quaint place, but all over the world. I know you, Aaron and Wayne are all non-believers, and I honour that, because frankly, I have found much more honour among atheists than among Christians. I judge a person not by their words but by their deeds. I know all three of you have not just spoken of honour, but practiced it. That is more than you can say of most believers."

Stars lit the sky like twinkling fireflies, but appeared still like an old black and white photograph that had turned grey. Lynton smiled, feeling the light breeze blow her hair gently in the moist night air. No matter where she was or whom she was with, she occupied a space like she owned it. Her smooth, long strides and determined manner were a compliment to Jesus, who had the same air of assurance that indicated an individual of supreme confidence. For Lynton, her manner of fearless poise and firm fortitude made one believe she could be riding a comet streaking to the limits of the known universe. She could make the stars move, the galaxies tumble and dart. But for now, with her right hand wrapped around Jesus' bent left arm, as they strolled up the street they were two imposing figures in a time of anxiety and confusion. Looking at the two of them would make even the most ardent villain shiver in dread.

Lynton asked if she could drop Jesus off at his boarding house, but he declined, saying that walking gave him a chance to think. They bade each other good night, and as Jesus walked briskly along First Avenue, he thought back on all the trials and tribulations that he had suffered in trying to get people to throw off their chains and take a stand against authority. How many times had he exhorted the peasant class to rise up and shed their chains?

He knew the world was a complacent place for the poor. They had always been the fodder for capitalism's cannon. All the work is done by those who receive no reward, while those who direct the work from their luxurious abodes reap the elaborately luxurious benefits.

The poor are the seeds that are put into the ground, and when the crop springs forth it is the poor who bring in the harvest, but again receive no reward. The best of the world are sucked up in the machinery of exploitation.

Sometimes the poor growl, shake themselves and spatter their blood for history in protection of the very system that exploits them. Their sacrifices for the good of humanity are forgotten by those arrogant purveyors of deceit who never shed their own blood, but rather, rest in ostentatious excess, raking in the bounty while others die for nothing.

The weariness of the struggle weighed heavily upon Jesus' psyche. He often felt as if his efforts fell upon the deaf ears of those who could not see the folly of their meagre existences, because they were too busy trying to pay for a home they could not afford, a car that was more then basic transportation, a giant screen television or the latest in name brand clothing. It was once said by a capitalist that if you couldn't buy happiness, then you were shopping in the wrong store. That described the folly of modern man, who simply had fallen prey to the culture of greed.

His weariness over how difficult it was to foment revolution still never stayed his efforts to stir up rebellion, but he knew rebellion was a fleeting idea, as people grew weary of always losing the battle against authority. He was weary himself, because the vast array of weapons used by the privileged class made rebellion almost impossible. And now he was also battling an evil

J. Wayne Frye

that was hell-bent on bringing about more than just economic mayhem. He looked at the porch of the boarding house, walked up to the steps and sighed. There to his right, on the far side of the porch in almost total darkness was the figure of a man he could not make out.

The figure, in an almost whisper said, "Bet you are glad to be home. You look tired. Must have had a hard night?"

Jesus, now recognizing the person by his voice, replied, "The night sometimes traps you in darkness, and it seems the light of the next day is never going to come."

The commodore said, "The night I find very inviting. It offers a certain peace knowing that in the darkness you actually have a friend, something that will comfort you. I love darkness."

Then, much to the commodore's surprise, Jesus said, as he opened the door and looked back over his shoulder, something that truly unnerved him. "Those who love darkness have trouble with the light, because the light exposes them for what they are. And commodore, I know what you are."

Surely some revelation was at hand;
Surely the Second Coming was at hand.
Hardly was Jesus' words out,
When a soft whisper became a shout.

J. Wayne Frye   199

WHEN JESUS CAME TO LADYSMITH
TO BATTLE THE ANGEL OF DEATH

In his mind a vast image of mayhem formed,
As the commodore sensed a coming storm.
A gaze blank and hot as the noonday sun
Had materialized and worry had begun.

Jesus had the commodore's number.
Words like daggers tore the commodore asunder.
The darkness, though the commodore was sure,
Would protect him against a man so pure.

Jesus meandered up to his room, leaving the commodore to contemplate exactly what the next step might be in implementing a plan conceived with a group of people who had all assembled in Ladysmith for a grand purpose which they hoped would shake the foundations of order in the world.

Meanwhile, Lynton was on the phone with Wayne, being very careful to not mention the fact that Jesus was in town. She assumed not mentioning it was not really lying as long as he never asked. When Wayne then asked to speak to Aaron, she said, "Well, believe it or not, he is spending the night with a very lovely young lady named Nichola."

"That old lecher," replied Wayne. "I hope he doesn't have a heart attack."

Playfully teasing her beloved, Lynton said, "Well, if he does have a heart attack, he'll go with a smile on his face."

WHEN JESUS CAME TO LADYSMITH
TO BATTLE THE ANGEL OF DEATH

The next day, Aaron and Nichola met Lynton and Hobbs at Jack's for breakfast. Lynton, when no one else was looking, winked at Aaron in acknowledgement that he obviously had a wonderful interlude with Nichola. Jesus had told them that he had a lead to follow up on the Seven Seals and would catch up with them later.

Lynton turned to Aaron and said, "Perhaps it would help if we got some information on the owner of that house where Hobbs saw the dead man. We can check public records to see who owns it."

Aaron replied, "I know who owns it. The lady next door told me his name. It is Samael Azazel."

"Say it again. Are you sure the last name is Azazel?" asked Lynton.

"Very sure, yes."

"In my demon hunting, the name Azazel has come up often. I assume you are not aware of the name?"

Nichola surprisingly interrupted. "A fallen angel."

Lynton replied, "Yes, according to the Book of Enoch, he is a fallen angel. In the Bible, the name Azazel appears in association with the scapegoat rite; the name represents a desolate place where a scapegoat bearing the sins of the Jews during Yom Kippur was sent. During the second temple period, he appears as a fallen angel responsible for introducing humans to forbidden knowledge. His role as a fallen angel partly remains in Christian and Islamic traditions."

Nichola then said, "If anyone has seen the movie *Fallen*, the angel Azazel can inhabit the bodies of different people and wreck havoc on the world. In the King James version of the Bible, it is Aaron" she offered as she looked over at Aaron Adams and smiled, "not this Aaron, of course, who was told to offer a bull as a sin offering for himself, and that would make atonement for himself. He took two goats and set them before the Lord at the entrance of the meeting tent, and cast lots on the two goats, one lot for the Lord and the other lot for Azazel. Aaron then presented one goat on which the lot fell for the Lord, and offered it as a sin offering; but the goat on which the other lot fell was for Azazel to appease him."

Lynton and Aaron were not terribly surprised at the knowledge pouring forth from Nichola, who continued. "The Book of Enoch says that Azazel possesses the ability to corrupt the whole earth and that to him all sin can be ascribed."

Lynton said, "Your knowledge on the subject of Azazel is vast."

"Oh, I am sorry that I interrupted you. That was rude."

"No," replied Lynton, "please go on."

"Enoch portrays Azazel as responsible for teaching people to make weapons of war and teaching women to use cosmetics to be more alluring to men and thereby be seductresses. And there arose much godlessness, and people were obsessed with fornicating. They were led astray and became corrupt in all their ways. The corruption brought on by Azazel degrades the human race, and the four archangels (Michael, Gabriel, Raphael and Uriel) saw much blood being shed upon the earth and lawlessness being wrought. God sees the sin brought about by Azazel and has Raphael bind Azazel hand and foot and cast him into the darkness and make an opening in the desert and cast him therein, and place upon him rough and jagged rocks, and cover him with darkness, and let him abide there forever, and cover his face that he may not see light. Azazel's fate is foretold near the end of Enoch, where God says, 'On the day of the great judgement he shall be cast into the fire.' However, there are those who think that through the intervention of the devil that Azazel was freed and has wrought evil upon the earth ever since."

Ending, Nichola turned to Lynton and said, "Is that accurate?"

WHEN JESUS CAME TO LADYSMITH
TO BATTLE THE ANGEL OF DEATH

"Very precise," replied an unsurprised Lynton.

As they were leaving the restaurant, Hobbs caught a glimpse of a man driving up First Street. It was Lloyd Edison. It was then that he reiterated to Aaron about the strange happenings the night he was in the bedroom with Edison, where it was learned that his brother had been killed on the beach in Victoria.

Aaron told Lynton and Hobbs to go to city hall and find out when Samael Azazel purchased the property, while he and Nichola went by the police department to find out more about Edison's brother's death. He asked if Hobbs knew his name.

"I am not sure. Obviously, his last name was Edison . It was Robert. I am pretty sure."

"When you saw Lloyd Edison that night, what was his reaction when told of his brother's death?

"Zilch, nothing – no emotion whatsoever."

Aaron took a deep breath. "And do you think he knew that shadow was there?"

"Never thought about it, but yes, I think he did. Definitely, I think he did. When I left, right before I noticed the shadow, his eyes were trained to the side, to his left. Although he did not move his head, his eyes were definitely peering to his left, as if he could see the shadow, too. Yes, I definitely feel he knew it was there. Yes!"

"O.K., I'll check with the RCMP and get back to you. You guys check on Azazel."

The astute and perceptive Aaron looked over at Lynton as he left, and he could tell exactly what she was thinking in regards to what he was looking for at the police station. If it was what she thought it was, then there would be a tie-in between the Victoria killing and the Ladysmith murder.

Nichola reached out and took Aaron's hand as they walked the few blacks to the RCMP office. As usual with police, there seemed resentment that someone would dare ask them for information. The person at the reception desk, who was ensconced behind bullet proof glass, glared at Aaron with disdain for expecting her to do her job – serve the public.

After her refusal to offer any information, which was supposedly available for public consumption, Aaron demanded to see the duty officer. She reluctantly complied with his request. Having on a uniform, for far too many people, seems to elevate the level of arrogance, as they hide their inadequacies behind a badge which they assume gives them the authority to be jerks. The cords of muscle knotting the sergeant's neck and straining the shoulder seams of his shirt, which was tenuously buttoned across a bulging chest made thicker by a bullet proof vest, was a way of saying, "I am an entitled member of society and have complete authority over you." He was two halves, one all-knowing and powerful, and the other, effectively hidden, was a scared man who needed a uniform and badge to validate his existence.

Aaron, of course, was not intimidated. He politely asked to know the details of what happened in regards to the murder of a man in Victoria called Robert Edison.

"I see no reason why you should be privy to that information," the sergeant said with glaring eyes that peered through the bullet proof glass with laser-like precision.

Aaron lifted his head. His high cheekbones and symmetrical features showing no acquiescence to any form of arrogance sent his way. He was still slender despite his years, toned and not at all stooped. He did not cower in fear like so many who came face to face with a policeman. Around Aaron's eyes were lines in just the right amount. It was probably obvious that he was probably predisposed to happiness, but at that moment he was deadly serious, and it showed in every fibre of his body. He gave the sergeant the patented crooked smile and said, "Privy to information that is available to the public based upon freedom of information? I think any citizen is entitled to that."

With a scowl, the sergeant replied, "You are not a Canadian citizen. I can tell by your accent you are an American."

Smiling, Aaron offered a direct answer that cut to the crux of what was a worldwide opinion towards Americans. "I am afraid you are correct, and frankly, with the current state of affairs, I am ashamed of that fact. I am not your typical arrogant American. I can assure you. All I want is just a bit of information to help me with a case I am working on."

"Private investigator, uh?"

"I am. Yes. And," Aaron said as he looked at Nichola, "she is a Canadian, so that should work."

"We don't allow concealed handguns in this country. We got some common sense about guns here."

"I appreciate that," said Aaron as he pulled back his suit jacket to show he had no concealed weapon. "The USA could use some common sense gun control, but, unlike Canadians, they think the right to pack a rod is God-given and you know how Americans snap to attention when the flag is waved or when Jesus is mentioned."

WHEN JESUS CAME TO LADYSMITH
TO BATTLE THE ANGEL OF DEATH

The sergeant lost his arrogant facade as a result of Aaron complimenting Canadians and their common sense approach to gun laws, as well as there lack of patriotic servitude and religious subterfuge. He said to Aaron, "That's unusual, an American with some sense about guns and religion."

"Well, I am not the usual American, fortunately. Do I get the info? Maybe even a look at the case file if that is permissible?"

"Your name and could I please see your P.I. licence?"

"I am Aaron Adams," replied Aaron as he reached inside his coat pocket to take out his P.I. licence.

Impressed, the sergeant quickly waved off looking at the ID, and said, "Heard of you. Who hasn't in this small town? Wayne Frye has made you famous."

"Don't believe everything you read," offered Aaron.

The now admiring sergeant said, "Hey, if 25% of what he writes is accurate, then you got my respect."

"Thank you."

WHEN JESUS CAME TO LADYSMITH
TO BATTLE THE ANGEL OF DEATH

The sergeant leaned on the counter and said, "There is a limit to what I can share with you, but I'll connect to the Victoria data system and give you what I can."

"Appreciate it."

The sergeant sat down by the computer and started typing. Nichola reached down and grabbed Aaron's hand as she whispered, "You're my new hero."

He whispered to her, "I am definitely no hero. Most heroes are dead. After last night I found out that I am really alive, more alive than I thought possible."

She had to say nothing in reply, because her twinkling eyes and knowing smile said it all. As she stood staring at him, the sergeant said, "Crime time is estimated at approximately 1:00 AM. Body was discovered on an isolated area of the beach in Oak Bay area of Victoria."

Aaron asked if there was anything unusual about the condition of the body. The sergeant took a deep breath, leaned forward and said, "I'll deny I ever told you this, because it is supposed to be information we are withholding for investigative reasons. The murder was committed with a long blade, very long and very sharp. The M.E. says it could have been a scythe – whatever that is."

WHEN JESUS CAME TO LADYSMITH
TO BATTLE THE ANGEL OF DEATH

"A long instrument that was once one of the most important of all agricultural hand tools, consisting of a curved blade fitted at an angle to a long, curved handle and used for cutting grain. But there is something else isn't there?"

"Well, yes there is but I am not at liberty to divulge that information as it is being held back for the same reasons, but I'll just say there was something missing from the body and leave it at that."

Aaron, without hesitation, said, "The heart?"

Shocked, the sergeant said, "How'd you know that?"

Smiling, as he turned to leave, Aaron said, "I'm a trained detective."

When they got outside, Nichola quizzically asked, "For real, how did you guess the heart was missing?"

"There is a pattern to all this. You see; Hobbs just saw Lloyd Edison ride by us this morning. A few days ago he was present when a supposedly ill Edison received information about the murder of his brother. Edison showed no emotion, and when Hobbs started to leave he saw a strange shadow on the balcony. Hobbs also saw the same figure at the top of those stairs in the house where he discovered a body with the heart missing. Just a bit of deductive reasoning, because the missing hearts are being used as part of some type of diabolical ceremony by what I would term a coven of evildoers, a group of people who are preparing for some type of cataclysmic incantation to bring about monumental evil."

"You are amazing Aaron. Your deductive abilities are uncanny."

"Of course they are. I know things about you that would amaze you."

Quizzically, she replied, "Really?"

"Oh yes. You see, after your little rendition about Azazel in Jack's you confirmed something Lynton and I had discussed earlier. In fact, I spent almost twenty minutes on the phone with her this morning while you were taking a shower and getting ready. We have concluded that with the name Nichola, you are most likely a member of the organization called the Order of the Hatchet. Are you and Jesus working in concert?"

Surprised, but not shocked, Nichola said, "Well, I must admit to having never met Jesus before, and frankly I do not put any credence whatsoever in him being the man from the Bible. I am not a believer, but I do believe there is evil all about, and good people must confront it."

WHEN JESUS CAME TO LADYSMITH
TO BATTLE THE ANGEL OF DEATH

Smiling, Aaron said, "So, you are truly a member of the Order of the Hatchet?"

"I'll neither confirm nor deny. How is that Mr. Detective?"

"That's fine my dear. Let's find Lynton and Hobbs to see what they have come up with."

Jack's was now their office, and as Lynton sat down Aaron gave her a little wink, which she assumed indicated that she and Aaron were right about Nichola being a member of the Order of the Hatchet. Jesus walked in and took a seat. He smiled at his cohorts and said to Aaron and Lynton, "so you two found out Nichola is a member of the Order of the Hatchet. Good work."

They both shook their heads, surprised that Jesus had known all along. Still, why should they have been surprised? He often jokingly said, "I know everything."

Hobbs, flabbergasted by the revelation, sat quietly in the realization that he was among people with incredible minds. He felt relieved that he had them on his side.

Aaron asked Lynton what she and Hobbs had found out about the person named Samael Azazel, and what she had to say was going to be a shocking revelation. "He has been in town off and

J. Wayne Frye

on for two years. He bought the house for cash, and has paid the taxes on time each year and has been twice cited for violation of ordinances in regards to untidiness."

Jesus jokingly said, "Must be evil then, because cleanliness is next to godliness."

All there got a smile on their faces as Lynton continued. "The problems were immediately fixed for the most part, but they took time, because he was out-of-town frequently. I asked her how she knew that, and she said because he told her, and that when city inspectors, who were called by the next door neighbour with numerous complaints, came to the house there was never anyone who answered the door. They would go back many times and never find anyone home. It sometimes took months for them to ever find someone there. Apparently, he was out-of-town more than he was in-town. We found thanks to that chatty clerk at city hall who said she was always frightened when he would come in to pay his taxes. She said that there was a dark nature to him, as he would always stand outside the doorway and wait until nearly 4:30, which was closing time; before he would come in, always making sure she and he were the only ones in the office. Then, the most unusual thing of all was that taxes are paid in the summer, and he always had a hooded jacket on with the hood pulled up and cinched so it completely covered his face."

J. Wayne Frye 213

Aaron then said, "But the clincher is where the tax notice was mailed, right?"

"So right, they were sent to Samael Azazel in care of a person staying at the Jenks' Boarding House.

"Commodore Ray!" interjected Jesus.

"You got that right," replied Lynton.

WHEN JESUS CAME TO LADYSMITH
TO BATTLE THE ANGEL OF DEATH

Chapter 10
There is No One in This Grave

I bury the dream that shines.
Black fire is my home.
I am the destroyer.
I am the destroyer.

I dwell in the black pit,
Where on a dark throne I sit.
I am the black angel of wrath.
I am the black angel of wrath.

On a deep and wide muddy path,
On a steep slope of a black road,
I am the destroyer.
I am the destroyer.

J. Wayne Frye   215

WHEN JESUS CAME TO LADYSMITH
TO BATTLE THE ANGEL OF DEATH

I bury the dream.
I spread my dark wings.
Black fire, red fire!
I am the destroyer.

How profound the mystery of the invisible is. We cannot fathom it with our miserable senses. Our eyes are unable to perceive what is either too small or too great, too near to or too far from us. We can see neither the inhabitants of a far away planet nor what organisms are in a drop of water. Our ears deceive us, for they transmit to us the vibrations of the air in sonorous notes. Our senses are fairies that work the miracle of changing movement into noise, and by that metamorphosis give birth to music, which makes the mute agitation of nature a harmony. Explanations then are often beyond human ability. Was what happened in that house and on that beach beyond explanation?

Perhaps that is why a restless night lay before poor Hobbs, as he tossed and turned on his hotel bed, staring up at the ceiling. He was scared. He got up and checked the lock and bolt of the door. He opened the drawers of the chest and looked under the bed. He listened, but for what? How strange it was that a simple feeling of discomfort, of impeded or heightened circulation, perhaps the irritation of a nervous center, a slight congestion, a small disturbance in the imperfect and delicate functions of his living machinery turned the poor

J. Wayne Frye

man into such a melancholy state. Then, he lay back on the bed and impatiently waited for sleep as a man might wait for the executioner. He waited for its coming with dread, and his heart beat rapidly and his legs trembled, while his whole body shivered beneath the warmth of the bedclothes, until the moment when he suddenly fell asleep, as a man throws himself into a pool of stagnant water in order to drown. He did not feel the perfidious sleep coming over him as usual, but a sleep which was close to him and watching him, which was going to seize him by the head, close his eyes and annihilate him.

Each day we all deal with evil, the evil of a world that has been turned over to corporations and the wealthy to destroy hope. A large part of this evil is the acceptance of wickedness in the cloak of religion by those who stand in church pulpits and point the finger of condemnation. People are searching for meaning in their lives of quiet desperation, and in the process they turn their minds over to charlatans in ecclesiastical robes of dishonour. Jesus had migrated from New Jersey to the Black Hills to Canada in a desperate attempt to save humanity from itself, and he always met with resistance from those who feared his message of acceptance and inclusion. He was a threat to the order of things that kept the common man locked in a prison of failed promises, so as Hobbs tossed and turned in his bed, Jesus was staring out his window at Jenks' Boarding House.

WHEN JESUS CAME TO LADYSMITH
TO BATTLE THE ANGEL OF DEATH

It is not unusual for those who have a message of hope to be labelled malcontents. Jesus was used to being put in prison for his devotion to the downtrodden and forgotten. He was used to condemnation, used to crying in the wilderness as the very people he tried to help condemned him. He had come to Ladysmith, because he had trailed an evil entity that was in search of the Seven Seals in order to unleash mayhem on mankind. His friend Aaron Adams was there by chance, but there would be those who would say that there is no chance in the circle of life, only lost opportunity. Over the many years, wandering in the wilderness of compliancy practiced by those who lined up for their own balls and chains, how many opportunities had he lost?

As he stared into the darkness he reflected on how his battles against evil always ended in catastrophe for him and those he tried to help, because he had been crucified so many times in so many ways in so many places. Lesser men would have given up the fight, as so many had, given up and accepted their fate by acquiescing to their own slavery to a system that had no heart and no soul, a system that ground people up in the grist mill of life.

He was weary and tired. At the same time, he was hopeful, because he had come across some others, who like him, were intent on making a stand against evil.

WHEN JESUS CAME TO LADYSMITH
TO BATTLE THE ANGEL OF DEATH

To sin by silence, when there should be protest makes cowards out of people. The human race has climbed on protest. Had no voice been raised against injustice, ignorance and inequities, the inquisition yet would serve the law and the gallows decide the least disputes. The few who dare must speak and speak again to right the wrongs of a society governed by those who sit on thrones of privilege. Press and voice must cry loud disapproval of existing ills, must criticize oppression and condemn the wealth-protecting laws that shield the privileged class from paying their fair share while letting the poor, with their toil and struggle, live in the squalor of poverty caused by greed. He knew he was a voice crying in the wilderness, but he was unable to cease railing against anyone who calls a land free that holds one fettered slave to greed. Until the manacled wrists of economic slaves were loosed to toss away the burden of poverty, until the soil upon which all trod was rescued from the clutch of corporations and awarded to labouring men and women he could not rest in peace. Until the evil that was let loose in Ladysmith was staid, he would fight to corral the evil that had been promulgated by those in service to darkness.

In Nichola's apartment, the elderly Aaron was staring at the ceiling at the same time Hobbs was. With the vibrant young women sleeping in his arms, he felt a new zest for life and for her. His shoulder was a respite from strife when you couldn't stand alone, but afterward he expected you to build inner strength, resilience, and to not expect flowers on birthdays, gifts at Christmas or impulsive purchases, because commercialism left him cold and indifferent. His relationship currency was a hug, careful words and thoughtful deeds that you could lock in a vault of hope. Nichola, who had been on a lonely journey all her life, had found someone who made her feel safe in a world where safety was a rare commodity.

Back at her house high on a mountain overlooking the Georgia Strait, Lynton was unable to sleep as she lay in bed thinking about her dear Wayne who would be upset with her for once again getting involved in demon hunting in a world he said was filled with so many demons that she was overwhelmingly out numbered, because the demons were not some supernatural entity but the living and breathing mortals who preyed upon the working men and women to pile up wealth and privilege in a world ruled by greed that rewarded the few at the expense of the many. Unlike her, he was a pessimist and saw the world through the lens of a sceptic, while she was able to find good among the vast evil that permeated a world that had been askew since man walked out of the ocean onto dry land.

Lynton's strength actually had been born of what many would consider a weakness, for she had known the terrible bite of poverty. When others would have given into despair, she rose from the ashes of misery. She, through determined tenacity, found strength. All along she was able to turn outward, expressing love to the world in the hope of some of it coming back. She offered the soul of persistence and resolve like a brilliant white light, a force to heal an ailing world of cynicism. Yet, there were the minions of despair who saw her kindness as a wounded side and pushed to take advantage of her, but that survival instinct to fight adversity made her unwavering in a commitment to righteous indication toward those who dared embrace the dark side. She understood that to help others she had to believe in herself. And so she took love and let it pour outward while it flowed in her own veins, channelling the spirit of the lioness in defence of her den. She could take any adversity and turn it into an advantage. She believed that when the darkness was overpowering you had to hold on to the last of the light, and know that when it is gone the darkness cannot defeat you, because when you burn you will rise from the ashes and you can do what no one else can, and through the pain you can stand up when others stay down. Out of her troubles and pain, she always, despite scars, emerged the strongest of souls capable of making the burning evil shriek with terror before her determination. She possessed the passion of a raging tempest. She believed in standing firm, in rising after every shattering blow, in never bowing before the evil of complacency.

J. Wayne Frye   221

WHEN JESUS CAME TO LADYSMITH
TO BATTLE THE ANGEL OF DEATH

This was the confidence of the phoenix, of one who has suffered into the ash of anguish, being reborn in the flames of hot pain and commanded to rise above misery and hopelessness. This was confidence hard-won yet deep, anchored in the true self that is always safe at the core, able to weather the storm. It is that which grows within, purging what was born of fear, clearing the way for love to grow, to take up every aspect Lynton embraced. And in this rawness, in this absolute vulnerability she found Wayne, found someone who needed her light to shine in the darkness of his life which had been torn asunder by another woman whom he had deeply loved, but who had betrayed him. She had been betrayed by lovers many times and was on the verge of giving up herself when she found someone who needed a lift even more than she did.

It was as if she had been a boat at sea, searching for safe harbour. Then one day she realized that she had become the safe harbour and could provide shelter for Wayne who had been frightened by the storm of life. To be strong was her choice, not just for herself but for him. She knew being strong wasn't being free of fear, quite the opposite. Strong was seeing all the issues and problems with no self deception, no soft filters. It was feeling the anxiety in full measure, acknowledging the fear, and still making the right choices. It was owning your errors and using them to make yourself a better person; and thereby, making others realize that there could be light in the darkness.

She had heard her pessimistically oriented husband quote Sartre, who said that over every person's life, Satan's fallen angels disperse from a black cloud the essence of evil, hoping that man's natural instincts will embrace evil out of universal selfishness. Thus was the eternal battle between good and evil, a battle in which evil usually was triumphant. However, evil rarely came up against the likes of Lynton Viñas and Aaron Adams, who, along with their intrepid cohorts were now preparing for battle. The sun rose on a new day and the warriors were ready for war!

As they sat at their usual table at Jack's, they all were worried about the fear that appeared to be gripping Hobbs. It was Jesus who said, "Calvin, I had a friend named Luke who once shivered with fear, and I said unto him, 'Do not worry about your life, what you will eat; or about your body, what you will wear. Life is more than food, and the body more than clothes. Consider the ravens: they do not sow or reap, they have no storeroom or barn; yet they find sustenance. Who, by worrying, can add a single hour to his life?' Put your fears aside my friend and face what lies ahead with the assurance you can weather any tempest, and though you might be defeated, in the end you will be triumphant in standing against adversity, triumphant in conquering fear."

"I am lucky to have found so many friends who are willing to stand by me," replied Hobbs.

"Remember Calvin that we are also here on a mission to procure the Seven Seals. Those seals and your problem are intertwined. We solve your problem, and we also solve the problem of the Seven Seals," offered Lynton.

Nichola said, "I feel there is some thing tracking our movements, some thing that wants to keep us from that house, some thing not living."

Aaron, being careful not to denigrate her assessment of the situation, said, "If there are other beings besides ourselves on this earth, how come no one has categorically proved their existence, been able to film them, been able to speak with them? I say worry about the living, not the departed or some supposed incarnation."

Jesus said with conviction, "Do we see every part of what exists? For example there is the wind, which is the strongest force in nature. It knocks down men and blows down buildings, uproots trees, raises the sea into mountains of water, destroys cliffs and casts great ships onto the breakers; it kills, it whistles, it sighs, it roars. But have you ever seen it, and can you see it? Yet it exists, and everyone knows it."

"Well put," offered Lynton.

J. Wayne Frye

WHEN JESUS CAME TO LADYSMITH
TO BATTLE THE ANGEL OF DEATH

Jesus, with his usual rhetorical flourish, said, "There is no evil book about how to be evil and how to be bad, because one is not needed. Why? Because the Bible is filled with more evil than any book ever written, and much of that evil is promulgated by a vengeful God in the Old Testament. The truth is evil prances about in disguise. You see, the devil doesn't come dressed in a red cape and with pointy horns. He sits behind an expensive desk in a board room and practices evil in a pinstripe suit by using a pen and legalese to steal and destroy any semblance of good."

Hobbs was still wondering where all this philosophical rambling was leading when he said, "So, am I a victim of evil or I am part of the evil?"

Aaron said, "You have been used in my opinion." He then took out his phone and called the local RCMP, asking for the desk sergeant, who immediately recognized his voice.

To everyone's great surprise, he asked a question that raised a red flag. "So sergeant, can you tell me one thing about the body of Robert Edison. Was it cremated?"

"Not sure. However, something like that would be matter of public record."

"Oh, I wasn't sure of that," replied Aaron. "I can check on line."

"May be too soon for it to be posted," offered the sergeant. "Let me check for you. Give me a sec."

While Aaron was waiting for the sergeant to check data on the computer, Lynton said, "I think I know where you are going with this."

Aaron smiled and said, "You're a very smart woman."

"Buried, no cremation," offered the sergeant.

"Have anything on where he was buried?" asked Aaron.

They could not hear the reply but Lynton instinctively knew what it was as Aaron said, "Thank you so very much, sergeant. I really appreciate it."

Lynton said, "He was buried in Ladysmith, right?"

"You bet."

Taking a deep breath, Lynton said, "There is one cemetery in Ladysmith. Now, you want to check the grave, because you do not think he was buried. There is only an empty grave. Right?"

"Right on the mark."

WHEN JESUS CAME TO LADYSMITH
TO BATTLE THE ANGEL OF DEATH

Hobbs, quizzically asked, "What does that have to do with what happened in that house?"

"Be patient," offered Aaron. "Everything is falling into place." He then looked at Jesus and said, "And your precious Seven Seals is tangled up in all this."

Jesus replied, "Yes, and if we solve Calvin's mystery, we'll get a good bead on where the seals might be." For some reason, he then looked directly into Nichola's eyes without uttering a word, but you could sense that he knew she was harbouring a secret, a secret that she felt a necessity to even keep from her new lover, Aaron. A secret that was carried, not out of maliciousness, but out of tenacious dedication to a cause, a cause that had been passed on from one generation to another through time.

"We meet at sundown," said Aaron.

"At the cemetery," interjected Lynton.

"At the cemetery," replied Aaron.

The environs of the cemetery were twisted like contorted bones, writhing in a silent scream. Upon the earth lay the cold stones, each marking a dwelling place in which no one is truly home. In the fast gathering darkness, the immaculately manicured ground and the outline of tombstones were dancing to the slow waltz of eternity. When the gate squeakily opened, it was with an announcing call to the dormant there to prepare for visitors in a place of darkness. The grass was already beginning to frost over, and there was no wind, no stars above, just blackness. Ahead of them the path glistened like white quartz. It was as if Aaron instinctively knew where the grave was, as they passed tombstones with flowers placed in reverence to those who had departed, leaving behind people who grieved. Of course, there were mostly flowerless tombstones as death is a condition that grows in acceptance as the years pass, because over time people move on with their lives and the tribulations of living. Love is a thing which lives even after death, and no amount of flowers or tears will fill the void left by those who pass on. People do not come to cemeteries for the dead. They come for the living. They come to embrace that which can be no more. What good does it do to talk to a withering, decomposing body? Is the proximity to the dead simply a brief moment in time where the living can still fill the love of the departed?

Nichola reached down and took Aaron's hand. Was she afraid? No, Aaron sensed she was only, in this place of death, wishing to feel close to the one for whom she now had so much affection. Proximity to death makes the living more aware of how important life and love are in a world where death is always waiting to claim another victim.

WHEN JESUS CAME TO LADYSMITH
TO BATTLE THE ANGEL OF DEATH

Unlike the bones that decayed beneath the surface, the tombstones weathered slowly, only their lettering showing the signs of the passing of time. As Nichola passed them, she occasionally touched one as she went by like her own heart was buried along with the dead. It seemed as if she had a connection to the dead.

On the other hand, Jesus seemed not sullen at all, but appeared to be at peace with the fact these people were now free of the trials and tribulations of life. To Jesus, graveyards were actually a place of new life where blossoms bloomed from the budding plant of renewal. The graveyard was a place to bring the joy of rebirth and renewal to the spirit in an onward voyage. He knew that in this thing called life there were monsters, evil angels that will keep you hemmed in a prison of hopelessness. It was the rich and powerful who were the guards of that prison. They were the evil that permeated all the earth and tried to garner all the good for themselves, while denying others the fruits of their individual labour. It was his mission to bring hope to those hopeless ones, joy to those joyless ones.

They came to a plastic marker that read: *Robert Edison*. It had the birth date and the date of death only. It was too early for a tombstone to be in place. They all stood there staring at the plastic marker. Aaron paced up and down. He looked at the others and gleamed with revelatory delight.

Lynton, realizing what Aaron had discovered, said, "The grass has not been disturbed. The ground has not been turned. There is no one in this grave."

Chapter 11
Ensnare in its Web of Evil

Mortal, mock not the Angel of Death,
Life is short and soon will fail,
And the fire everlasting
Is no idle fairy-tale.

"The number seven corresponds to the seven spirits of God, and the sevenfold nature of the divine order in the world. As each of the Seven Seals is opened in turn, the events and catastrophes leading to the dissolution of the world are set in motion. It is my purpose in finding them to prevent them from being opened before the time they are supposed to be revealed, a time when humanity is to end," said Jesus.

J. Wayne Frye   231

WHEN JESUS CAME TO LADYSMITH
TO BATTLE THE ANGEL OF DEATH

"I think that is malarkey," offered Aaron, "but I will grant you that whoever is involved with this murder is also involved in trying to find the Seven Seals, because these miscreants are as delusional as you are. Those seals, I am certain, are right here in Ladysmith. I am sure these devil worshipping degenerates believe the location will somehow be revealed through some type of abominable ceremony. Furthermore, I believe that Hobbs is somehow necessary for this ceremony that may be planned or maybe was already performed, which is why he was in that house. He was hypnotized and through post-hypnotic suggestion he was vital to this whole ceremony, so vital that he was lured into that house for some unknown reason. He was allowed to live, perhaps because his function in this whole diabolical scheme is yet to reach fruition."

As they turned to exit the graveyard, Nichola looked to her right at a very unusual gravestone. She stood as if hypnotized, just staring as a slight shiver enveloped her body. There was a cruel irony in the gravestone. It was there with its stone cold glow. It was strong, erect and ready to last a hundred years more. What was under it had already perished and begun the inevitable decaying process many years ago. Still, the huge stone monument with a beautiful young girl lying in repose on a stone bed was a permanent reminder to mark something as transient as life. The flesh below, devoured by worms and irreversibly rotted with time had returned to the soil, the memories had all evaporated into the mists of time; a life had been long ago extinguished. Mourners had probably visited this cold stone as if time and the person below had been halted in what never can be permanent. All life must eventually be extinguished. The stone was something simply to visit when loved ones left behind could not bear the separation any longer. Yet, all who visited would eventually wind up the same way as that thing beneath the stone. However, for a while, at least, it offered something tangible and dependable when all else was in turmoil. The loved one had departed, but the stone stayed as a cold reminder of that fleeting thing called life.

Jesus, seeing that Nichola was feeling a surge of emotion put his arm around her shoulder and whispered, "A person's life should never be marked by a gravestone, something so cold and immobile. Perhaps a tree with a wind-chime in the branches could do more justice, or a simple song sung into the breeze. What lies in the ground was only flesh and blood. That is never what a person was. Hopefully, the person below soared with the eagles on lofty breezes and swam in oceans deep. Or, perhaps the person that lies here had a life of terrible want and pain; a life filled with misery and now knows the freedom of death. Death is never to be feared. It is life which causes the most fear for all of us."

WHEN JESUS CAME TO LADYSMITH
TO BATTLE THE ANGEL OF DEATH

As they all filed out of the graveyard, Lynton lingered behind and read the barely discernable inscription on the huge stone monument at which Nichola had stared. It read:

Nichola Diane Lyle
Born March 15, 1926 – Died March 15, 1996
A Loyal Soldier in the Order of the Hatchet

Relative with the same name thought Lynton. Maybe? Or, was there something deeper, something more problematic related to that grave? She would let it go for the time being. There were more pressing matters.

Of all those there, Jesus had actually battled Satanic forces the most, and even he had usually come out on the short end. He never said directly that Satan existed, other than as a symbol of evil which was promulgated by the mortal beings who used him as a prop to extort money from non-thinkers who believed by tossing money in the collection plate they could buy their way into paradise. For that reason, he was quick to denounce the hypocrites who used religion to promote judgementalism and to get the gullible to follow those who proclaimed themselves superior interpreters of the word. In the process, he never claimed powers beyond those of an ordinary human being, but it was plain to see that his oratory skills elevated him to being every bit as effective as the Biblical Jesus in rousing an audience. He was a spellbinding oratory, which was the reason the power structure of both church and government feared him everywhere he went. Of course, he understood that fear made him highly vulnerable.

Nichola, who, as they were walking from the cemetery, summoned the courage to issue a sort of challenge to Jesus. She said, "Are you capable of stopping the evil going on here? Do you possess the power to intervene and let good triumph?"

"We all possess that power, Nichola. You should know that," he replied, giving her a knowing wink, as if he knew something about her that no one else did.

A kind of awe fell upon her when she heard him say that, and some trepidation accompanied that awe, because she was harboring a secret. She stoically thought to herself, "Could he know?"

WHEN JESUS CAME TO LADYSMITH
TO BATTLE THE ANGEL OF DEATH

As they all listened intently, Jesus said, "You must remember that we are all angels of one sort or another, but there is a fine line between good and evil, and angels must make a choice like all of us must. Satan is called an angel. So, angels can be good or evil. You may not believe in angels or in Satan and that is fine, but I am sure you all believe in good and evil. I am also sure, whether you are religious or not that you can see the Bible is nothing more than a book of allegories to make people think. Thinking, unfortunately today, is a lost art in world where the banality of modern communications, which is controlled by self-serving corporations, is utilized to make people let others, meaning the powerful and rich, do their thinking for them. You see, people capable of deductive and thoughtful reasoning are a threat to the power structure. Keep the easily manipulated entertained with nonsensical tripe and propaganda which turns their minds into mush. Actually make the poor believe they are only temporarily disadvantaged eventual millionaires, and they will blame themselves for their poverty rather than a system that oppresses them."

Aaron, as always, frustrated by Jesus' tendency to engage in rhetorical theatrics, shook his head and said, "What does this have to do with the task at hand, finding a way to explain Hobbs seeing a dead man who disappeared, and connecting that to the Seven Seals, which, according to you, must be found to stop Armageddon?"

WHEN JESUS CAME TO LADYSMITH
TO BATTLE THE ANGEL OF DEATH

Jesus, in his usual calm manner said, "That's my friend, Aaron. He is never patient, always in a hurry to solve a case. Be aware my friend that the entire world is sick with a terminal illness. Its fever spikes as those left behind by a cruel economic system cry for some compassion. The shortness of breath lingers as the system ignores those poor souls while a limited few live in luxurious excess. The world is strewn with the glass shards of lost hope and broken promises. This is the story of evil, and the evil can be in an economic system that crushes the poor and middle class under the jack-booted thuggery of corporations and the wealthy, or it can be the equal evil represented by those who relish doing heinous wickedness for the mere pleasure they derive from it. There are those who embrace evil as if it was an aphrodisiac of ecstasy. The evil ones are slow and methodical in the way they carry out their plans. They are more patient than the righteous. Be patient my friend. The answers to both mysteries are within our grasp."

Aaron did not reply, but rather, reflected on the simple idea that he genuinely felt Jesus too often turned every response into a sermon on the mount. He was an idealist, but Aaron knew idealists usually wound up dead, destroyed by the very people they were trying to help who were too moronic to realize they were lining up for their own balls and chains. Simply put, a thought was like a rifle, its usefulness depended on the intelligence of the user, and few people had the intelligence to see their own lunacy. It was obvious to Aaron that as long as there were ill-informed people supporting stupid governments, people would continue fluttering in the whirling cesspool of evil created by the powerful to control the masses. Part of that evil was right there in Ladysmith in the form of a heinous coven of despicable devil worshippers sternly bent on summoning the absolute vilest demons of evil represented by man's embrace of the dark side. He felt that if he solved the mysterious murder in that house things would miraculously fall into place and Hobbs' worries could be laid to rest in the bosom of tranquility. However, as always, the evildoers were shielded and protected by privilege.

The dark side of humanity had descended on Ladysmith and it was up to these intrepid defenders of righteousness to face-off against evil and bring the bright rays of warm sunshine into the cold dark abyss of wickedness. The problem with the vast majority of the world's inhabitants was that they failed to realize that standing against evil required a dedication most people could not fathom. Complacency and apathy makes frustrated people give up on the idea that the perpetrators of an economically evil system would ever be made to share their bounty. The truth is, the privileged class has never, nor will they ever, willingly accept a just system that creates fairness and justice for all people. That is why defiance is crucial.

Aaron, as a young man in the late 1960's, had joined the demonstrations to end an illegal and immoral war in Vietnam and to promote economic justice, but as he watched the ghettos of America going up in flames he finally, one lonely night, stood on a Harlem street, as the neighbourhood was engulfed in fires set by the people who lived there, decided that the poor were their own worst enemies. Why he asked, as he shouted at the rioters, were they burning down their own neighbourhood? His impassioned plea with the rioters was recorded by a CBS news crew as his anger boiled over into a rant that was played over and over again on the news: "Why are you doing this to your own neighbourhood? You are burning down public housing, places where people live in squalor, but still have a roof over their heads. Places where people raise families and struggle to put food on the table in a nation that has made poverty a crime. You are destroying mom and pop stores that provide your food in a neighbourhood that big chain stores avoid. You are destroying the homes of those who serve you. You don't see corporate headquarters here. You see human beings who struggle every day to survive in a nation with the biggest gap between the rich and poor in the First World. The people here deserve better than this. They get no compassion from a nation where greed is the religion of the privileged class. I understand your anger. But, this is not a protest. This is just anarchy with no purpose. You want to demonstrate. You want to burn, loot and pillage - take your anger out on the real culprits. Take your anger to Wall Street, to the corporate headquarters and to the gated communities where the barons of greed live in luxurious splendour. Those same barons of greed will be handed money by the government to rebuild what you have torn down. You are not winning by doing this. You are just lining the pockets of those who hold stock in corporations that will profit off your anger."

Aaron suddenly realized just how much he loved this man calling himself Jesus, loved his anger, his gall and his devotion to the rectification of the evil which permeated the entire world with an insidiousness that cut to the core of hope, destroying everything that stood in the way of the greed that wrapped the world in darkness. His blood now pumping with the hot blood of indignation, he turned to Jesus and defiantly said, "Let's get this show on the road. I am tired of screwing around. Let's take on these evildoers and bring down their wicked house of infamy and find those Seven Seals."

Jesus winked at Aaron and said, "That's my Aaron!" He then turned to Lynton and said, "So, you found out a lot about Samael Azazel did you? But there is one thing you did not research I am sure."

WHEN JESUS CAME TO LADYSMITH
TO BATTLE THE ANGEL OF DEATH

Of all those there, Jesus had actually battled Satanic forces the most, and even he had usually come out on the short end. He never said directly that Satan even existed, other than as a symbol of evil which was promulgated by the mortal blood suckers who used him as a prop to terrorize the ill-informed and to extort largesse from those non-thinkers who believed tossing money into the collection plate would keep him at bay and buy their way into paradise. For that reason, he was quick to denounce the hypocrites who used religion to promote judgementalism and to get the gullible to follow those who proclaimed themselves superior interpreters of God's word. In the process, he never claimed powers beyond those of an ordinary human being, but it was plain to see that his oratory skills elevated him to being every bit as effective as the Biblical Jesus in rousing an audience. He was an extraordinarily spellbinding oratory which was the reason the power structure of both church and government feared him everywhere he went.

Nichola, who, as they were slowly walking from the cemetery, summoned the courage to issue a sort of challenge to Jesus. She said, "Are you capable of stopping the evil going on here? Do you possess the power to intervene and let good triumph?"

"We all possess that power, Nichola. You should know that," he replied, giving her a knowing wink, as if he knew something about her that no one else did.

A kind of awe fell upon her when she heard him say that, and some genuinely concerned trepidation accompanied that awe, because she was harboring a secret. She stoically thought to herself, "Could he know?"

Jesus then turned to Lynton and said, "My friend Aaron is a non-believer who knows the Bible better than anyone I have encountered. Of course, he knows it just so he can point out all the inconsistencies and hypocrisy it contains. He has known all along about Azazel being a fallen angel who taught men to make swords, knives, shields and breastplates, and that it was he who promoted war as a solution to problems. So, I am sure he finds it interesting that the owner of that house carries the last name Azazel."

Lynton said, "Hey, I remember the name of the evil angel that inhabited the bodies of others in that Denzel Washington movie – *Fallen*. When I hear the name Azazel I must admit to trembling with trepidation. You are; thereby, insinuating that this Mr. Azazel may be capable of inhabiting the bodies of others, taking on their form in order to move about and sew the evil that has come to Ladysmith."

Jesus replied, "Evil takes many forms."

WHEN JESUS CAME TO LADYSMITH
TO BATTLE THE ANGEL OF DEATH

Aaron said, "Yeah, and whatever form it takes; in the end, evil is usually the victor. Evil has far more power than good."

Head bowed, Lynton, in an almost whisper, said "Azazel has never faced anyone like us before."

"We'll beat him this time," offered Nichola.

"Don't be so sure," said Aaron, as they walked through the cemetery gate.

There is a kind of quiver that trembles around through the body when you are contemplating something so strange and mesmerizing that it is actually a fearful joy to be alive, and you realize that you are about to go into a monumental battle. Your lips turn dry and your breath comes short, but you wouldn't be anywhere else or with anyone else, because the comradeship and the camaraderie elevate your spirit. This was one of those times!

A sudden shiver ran through them all, not a cold shiver, but a shiver of caution, and so they hastened their steps, uneasy at being in the gathering darkness, because it seemed as if they were being followed; that somebody or some thing was walking at their heels. They all periodically glanced over their shoulders but saw nothing behind them. The trees seemed to be dancing around them and the earth was heaving with fear. Still, they moved forward.

J. Wayne Frye   243

WHEN JESUS CAME TO LADYSMITH
TO BATTLE THE ANGEL OF DEATH

Hobbs was elated that he had found so many people willing to help him, even though they were also now involved in the search for the Seven Seals. His predicament and the search for the seals were inextricably intertwined. He was certain of that. He sometimes had thought that he was mad, absolutely mad, as if he was unable to fathom the situation and analyze it with the most complete lucidity. Had he simply been a reasonable man labouring under a hallucination? He considered the mere irrefutable fact that some unknown disturbance must have been excited in his brain, one of those disturbances which physiologists and psychologists of the present day try to note and to fix precisely, and that disturbance must have caused a profound gulf in his mind and in the order and logic of his ideas. Similar phenomena occur in dreams and lead people through the most unlikely real or imaginary images, without causing any surprise, because the verifying apparatus and sense of control have gone to sleep, while the imaginative faculty wakes and works. Was it not possible that one of the imperceptible keys of the cerebral finger-board had been paralyzed in him? Some men lose the recollection of proper names, or of verbs, or of numbers or merely of dates as a consequence of an accident. Was he in an accident that he had somehow forgotten, or was it true that he had been hypnotized and given a post hypnotic suggestion that led him to that infernal house owned by Samael Azazel, where that abominable creature had stood at the top of those stairs?

WHEN JESUS CAME TO LADYSMITH
TO BATTLE THE ANGEL OF DEATH

Jesus and Nichola were walking side-by-side and he whispered to her, "I do not have to find those seals, but I do need to know they will be safe from the Angel of Death that now stalks us. I know that it is you dear woman who is a member of the Order of the Hatchet and are here to spirit them away to safety, to find a safe haven where they will be protected from discovery by evil forces that desire to unleash Armageddon."

She said nothing. She only looked over her shoulder at Aaron, wanting to tell him the truth, tell him that her love for him was more real than anything she had ever experienced. She turned back toward Jesus and whispered, "They are hidden here in Ladysmith, but I do not know where. It is my mission to find them and take them to a safer place."

She thought back on what it was like to be with Aaron. There was something so warm, something that felt right, smelt right. She thought about how she let her body sag in his arms, her muscles become loose. He gave her the respect of an equal but cradled her like a cherished child. In that embrace she felt her worries lose their keen sting and her optimism raise its head from the depths of her constant pursuit of justice in an unjust world. She let loose for awhile the burden of her eternal commitment to an ideal that made her a servant to a mission handed down from forbearers who had served a just cause. Her body quivered as she reflected on the depth of love she had for a man old enough to be her grandfather. Perhaps she had, after so many years, lost the hope that had been there all along, but without some love had been trapped like crystals in a stone. She longed to feel his warmth, she had an intense desire to feel him once again gently brush her hair back with his rough, wrinkled fingers and gently kiss her. She slowed up, waited for him to catch up, reached down and gripped his hand. Her eyes turned to him with such softness the glare was like a soft blanket on a cold night that wraps you in its warmth.

Wherever the comrades went they sensed they were being followed by some unknown entity. They dared not look behind them at the being itself, whatever it was, but they did slowly take in glimpses of its shadow reflected on their left. The shadow had magnificent flapping dark wings, huge and bird-like, extending from its back. Even looking at the shadow, one could sense its glowing eyes that shined like beacons of evil against the grey of the sidewalk. The Angel of Death was stalking them.

The Angel of Death stalks with determination the righteous, while he exonerates and coddles the wicked, those who hurt others with cold indifference. The evil angel comes with fingers of knives to slice out the eyes of the righteous, who watch in terror the horror and pain implemented by callous minds intent on denying hope and justice. And when standing before the greedy, the false and mortal who crave power, the Angel of Death encourages them to show no pity, because to this angel there is beauty in the evil promulgated by the servants of Satan. Watching the righteous being slaughtered provides this hideous angel with glorious ecstasy.

This battle against evil was continuous for this man called Jesus. He saw people suffer, fall into confusion and become overwhelmed with fear and doubt. He understood personal guilt, for untold transgressions were a steady hindrance to the advancement of hope, because he realized the actions of a person cannot be undone. He knew the past was a burden that lay heavy on people with a conscience. Still, in his eyes, there was recognition that peace can be found among chaos. Jesus was a personal guide, the one to answer questions and quiet the soul. He could simply take your hand and explain what you needed to know. He knew that the battles of life in a cruel world with no heart or soul can break you and leave you for dead, but he also knew how to extend a hand to help you get up again. He knew that mankind needed to hope for the best, prepare for the worst and know that defeat happens more than victory, but the greatest defeat of all is giving up. Hope he saw as a bright star in a hopelessly dark universe. Through light years of distance, the brightness filled the inner self. Hope, he understood, was not just an emotion; it was a promise that giving up was not an option. When the fighter has been laid on the canvas by a well placed punch, hope is there saying, 'Get up! Take a nine count if you must, but be ready to stand, and have the ref wipe off your gloves. You can still win that match called life.' Hope is drawn to the person who sees beyond the present defeat, beyond the moment of being cast down, beyond the loss of so many battles, and beyond the negative words of hopeless voices. There is another voice that is emanating from the bright star beaming in the heavens telling you to look beyond the darkness to the bright light of sacred hope.

He saw in poor Hobbs that his current trouble was like an anvil of despair around his neck. To lift his sagging spirits he said, "You have the two best sleuths in the world to find out what really happened in that house. They have both been to hell and back many times in the pursuit of truth. They will not let you down. Be strong, and no matter what fate awaits, know that you have champions of hope in your corner."

The intrepid searchers for truth and justice suddenly heard a flapping of wings, and overhead the stars were blotted out by a giant creature, which flew over them toward the ocean. Creatures of the night rule a world trapped in darkness, but these champions of righteousness had the light of hope shining brightly in their eyes.

WHEN JESUS CAME TO LADYSMITH
TO BATTLE THE ANGEL OF DEATH

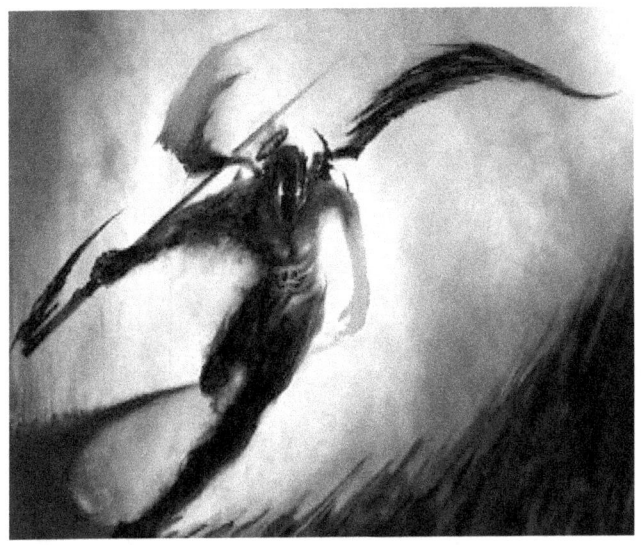

An incredible darkness fell upon the sky; the kind of darkness that robs you of your best sense and replaces it with a paralysing realization that evil is about. Their muscles became cramped and unable to move as they gazed at the creature seemingly capturing the heavens as the impending night descended on Ladysmith.

They only knew their eyes were still there, because they felt themselves blink, still instinctively moisturizing the organs they had no current use for. There was complete silence; not even the chirping of birds could be heard. They all knew that thing in the sky was looking for something called the Seven Seals, and that what happened to Hobbs in that house was somehow connected. That abomination soaring toward the bay was a despicable predator, a predator looking for souls to ensnare in its web of evil.

J. Wayne Frye

WHEN JESUS CAME TO LADYSMITH
TO BATTLE THE ANGEL OF DEATH

Chapter 12
His Little Headache

*It is when we face the moment
the worst of our kind can do,
that we then shudder to know
the horrible taint in ourselves
that awe cracks the mind's shell
and enters the beating heart,
not to flower, not to glow
but to bring evil from below.*

The next morning, Lynton and Aaron stood
undetected behind some playground equipment in
the small park across the street from the infamous
house where Hobbs had seen a dead body. They
had seen one man leave it; but all they could tell

of him was that he apparently wanted to hide his face, based upon the fact he was, even on a warm morning, wearing a hooded jacket that hid his profile from view. Interestingly, the man left the front door slightly ajar. It was then that Lynton said, "I'll follow him."

"Be careful. I don't want to get in any trouble with Wayne. He is going to chastise me enough for letting you get involved in the first place."

She smiled and nodded her head, her hair falling over her right eye as she crept out of the park. She loved this kind of thing!

Lynton's smile, thought Aaron, had to be distilled not just accepted. There was magic in it as if butterflies seemed to escape from the pit of her stomach and the sun had somehow toppled down from the sky and made a home right there in her heart. She had the kind of smile that made you feel happy to be alive and just a little bit more human for being allowed to bask in her glow. It was a smile you could put in your hip pocket and carry into eternity. The way her lips lifted upward. The way her little dimples crinkled. The way her teeth were sparkling white and perfectly aligned; the warm glow in her eyes that were part of the smile that displayed deep sincerity which oozed with bright rays of sunshine that warmed the soul of anyone lucky enough to be on the receiving end of that gorgeous display of specialness made the world seem a much better place. This was the woman who had given renewal to his biographer, Wayne Frye. And Aaron realized that he had also found renewal in his life, because he had found Nichola. Yet, there was something mysterious about her, something that he felt she was not sharing with him, something that Jesus knew about, too, but was also not sharing.

Aaron, instinctively felt inside his left coat jacket, as he always did when getting ready to face uncertainty in pursuit of criminal culprits. It was reassuring to know that he always had that big bad 45 to rely on in case things went south. He remembered what he once read in a Daschel Hammett novel about a P.I. knowing one important thing when on a case: "as soon as anyone said you didn't need a gun, you'd better take one along that worked." Of course, as he patted his left side for reassurance, he realized he was in Canada, and when you crossed the Canadian border sanity prevailed in regards to handguns. This was a nation, unlike the USA, with sane gun laws, where you didn't see arrogant, gun-loving fake patriots walking around Wal-Marts with AK-47's slung over their shoulders. For Americans, guns were a religion, an addiction just like alcohol, and alcohol was like love as it became a habit. The kind of habit where the first kiss is magic, the second is intimate, the third is routine, and for Americans guns were as routine as love. Discretion is the better part of valour, so

WHEN JESUS CAME TO LADYSMITH
TO BATTLE THE ANGEL OF DEATH

Aaron had not brought his gun to Canada. Anyway, if Jesus was right, a gun was a poor defence against the forces of evil he was going up against.

Aaron came out of hiding and moved toward the house. He had no idea what he was going to do, but he was determined to ring the doorbell and come face-to-face with Mr. Azazel, or whoever else might be in the house. What he might say he wasn't sure, but he'd go with the flow. The doorbell rang with a sombre tune, and he rang it again and again. There was no answer. He took a deep breath, looked around to see that the street and the porches of nearby houses were vacant. He pushed on the door and it slowly opened. He scurried in and quickly closed the door behind him.

Despite it being a bright day, all the curtains were closed and the house was dark. Thus, the rooms were draped in shadows. Aaron, a man used to the horrors of a world where cruelty was the norm rather than the exception, was sufficiently inoculated against the travesties of that world which was ruled by and for the privileged with no compassion for those lost in the daily struggle to keep their heads above water. That is why he was used to seeing the dark underbelly of a world that had no place for humaneness. Even religion was a cash and carry business, where if you tossed enough money in the collection plate your sins

J. Wayne Frye

were more readily forgiven than those of someone who could only manage to deposit a pittance. He was in the same room where Hobbs had seen the body. There, by the very sofa where that body had been placed, was a truly abominable sight. Aaron took a deep breath and moved closer. Immediately at his feet was the body of a man lying at full length upon the floor, his arms flung out on either side, and his white face with a look of horror frozen on it, and his features were gleaming dully in the unsteady light that was glistening through the partially opened curtain over the window.

He assumed he was dead and Aaron was so certain as to how he had died that without an instant's hesitation he dropped on his knees beside the corpse and reached down to pull back his suit coat. He gently pulled it back and there on the well-dressed person was a gapping hole where his heart used to be. What was discombobulating was the apparent state of the corpse. He had been dead for some time, probably days, but the smell of zinc sulphate, which Aaron was familiar with from visits to morgues, and tiny puncture wounds in the neck indicated that the zinc sulphate had been used in an attempt to preserve the body through injections of the chemical.

The corpse's eyes were black, the hair dark and very thick, and the skin was pasty white in colour. It was his intention to search for the strange weapon used to kill him, but he instinctively knew it had been a scythe. He immediately assumed that this man and the man Hobbs had seen were one and the same, a victim of a strange rite, because he peered over and saw the rug pulled back with the Baphomet image clearly visible. He then heard footsteps ascending the stairs, got up and walked to the hallway where he saw the back of what appeared to be a creature of immense bulk and height. It had wings on its back. He shouted, in hopes of halting the thing, despite knowing he had no gun, "halt or I'll shoot."

The creature did not turn but simply said in a reverberating voice that seemed to bounce off the walls of the house, "I am impervious to your feeble bullets."

The creature walked onto the top landing, turned right and bounded into a room. Aaron leaped the stairs two at a time and made it to the room, where he saw the creature go onto a balcony and leap down onto the yard far below. It was too much of a leap for Aaron, so he turned and ran down the stairs and out the front door. When he got to the side of the house and below the balcony, the thing was gone. Exhausted, as he was trying to catch his breath, he heard the back door slam shut and the sound of muffled voices. He mustered enough energy to rush to the back yard just in time to see a black SUV racing down the back alley. Now completely out of breath, somehow he managed the strength to rush back into the house and quickly dashed to the sofa area where the body had been. It was gone, along with any proof it was ever there. There was no need to contact the police, because like Hobbs, there was no way to convince the police that there had been a body on the floor. It had been spirited away by the people in that black SUV.

While Aaron was engrossed with the nefarious goings on in the suspect house, Lynton was engaged in the clandestine trailing of the mysterious figure that had left the house. With hood over his head, he had made his way down Buller Street, turning right onto First Street. He removed the hood and Lynton crossed the street to follow on the opposite side and noticed that he was a bit distinguished looking. His hair was done very nicely; he had some form of oil mixed in to give a short but noticeably wavy form to the greying strands. His forehead was almost square, large and imposing, and he had an air of authority in his deportment. A few lines were laid upon his brow, but they were dismissive as tricks of light in the morning sun.

He went into the famous Downtown Bakery Shop where he took a seat with a somewhat portly late middle-aged man. She took a seat at one of the sidewalk tables and observed through the large window the two men in a very animated conversation. The portly man had his back to her, so she could not make out his features, but she noticed the man she followed had eyebrows that tilted upward in a devilish sort of way, almost like horns. His eyes were made of rich mahogany. The eyes told of many secrets that were held locked in a strongbox so strong that you wouldn't dare to open it in fear of what you might find within. The most striking feature was the 1940's pencil-thin moustache. It highlighted the frown placed upon his mouth and somehow made him seem more authoritative than his aura already suggested. If one ventured close enough, his mahogany eyes would hungrily envelop yours and pull your feet towards him, so powerful was his gaze, almost as if he had the power of hypnotism. It was nothing he did precisely; it just looked as if he had a secret you would enjoy hearing about. He got up, left the shop and did not look at Lynton, who lowered her head to avoid eye contact. She continued to sit at the table until he got to the next street corner, then she got up and followed. He turned left onto the next street, which was Buller, and she instinctively knew he was headed back to that abominable house of evil. She scurried rapidly after him. She turned left onto Buller, and he had disappeared from the street. She looked toward the mystery house and saw a shadowy figure moving down the side of the house. She walked across the street and stood there waiting, not sure what she should do. After a few minutes, she heard the flapping of wings to the right side of the house and heard a commotion inside as if someone was scurrying about.

WHEN JESUS CAME TO LADYSMITH
TO BATTLE THE ANGEL OF DEATH

Just as she started toward the front door, Aaron walked out and said, "I saw a body, saw it on the floor by the sofa. Then I saw some creature like thing, maybe it was an apparition, leap off the balcony. I rushed down stairs and outside to pursue it. I made it to the back yard just as a black SUV sped down the alley. The thing, the man, whatever it was had disappeared. I went back into the house through the back door and the body was gone."

It was obvious that the man Lynton had followed back to the house was the same person or thing that Aaron had encountered at the top of the stairs. He had gone inside to distract Aaron while the dead body was spirited away.

Lynton told Aaron what had happened to her, as they walked back downtown to see if the portly man was still in the bakery. He was not, but somebody else was. There, at a table by the window was Jesus sitting with Nichola. Nichola had in front of her a thick plastic container. Jesus looked outside at Aaron, back at Nichola, gently touched her shoulder and got up. He walked outside and said to Lynton, "Come, let's walk while Nichola and Aaron say goodbye. She must immediately be on her way to secure the book of the Seven Seals."

Aaron, mystified and shocked, did not say a word as he rushed into the bakery and sat down across from Nichola. He stuttered a bit as he said, "What, what, what is this about you leaving?"

"I have no choice my darling. I must secure the Seven Seals from the Angel of Death. It is my duty as a member of the Order of the Hatchet."

Perplexed, Aaron said "My darling, I sensed you were a member of that organization, because my powers of deduction are fine tuned enough because of my profession to see things others do not. So, in that respect I am not shocked, as I assumed you would tell me about it in your own good time. Why you must you leave someone who has grown to truly love you."

"I love you, too. I will tell you what Jesus is, no doubt, sharing with Lynton right now, but I cannot tarry my dear, as time is not on my side, but the truth is I discovered where the seals were hidden. After much reflection this morning, I took Jesus to the cemetery here in town, as seeing my ancestor's grave there when we went to check Robert Edison's grave made me realize just where the seals might be."

She sighed and continued, "There, we removed the gold leafed book with the Seven Seals. It was hidden under the grave stone of my ancestor who brought the seals here in 1987. She, like I am, was a member of the Order of the Hatchet. She obviously arranged, once she knew death was

imminent, for the seals to be buried in a hermetically sealed solid plastic container under the stone by another member of the order. Ironically, it was buried right under the book that was in the right hand of the sleeping girl on the tombstone. The spot was obvious to anyone astute enough to look."

(The seals were buried in the ground near where the book is in the right hand of the sleeping girl.)

She continued, "The Order of the Hatchet, as has been the case all these years, is entrusted to keep the Seven Seals safe from those who want to unleash Armageddon. I must go before I am found by the coven and the Angel of Death that has performed the Rite of Judgement by having a man slay his brother as Cain slew Abel. The body Hobbs found was the preserved body of Robert Edison. Although there is no direct proof of it, he was killed by his bother, Lloyd. Hobbs saw the

WHEN JESUS CAME TO LADYSMITH
TO BATTLE THE ANGEL OF DEATH

Angel of Death outside the bedroom balcony when he visited Lloyd Edison, who was in bed recovering from what was supposed to be an illness. There was no illness. It was faked to lure Hobbs to his bedside. There Hobbs was hypnotized by Edison, who, according to what Jesus and I found through our research, was trained in hypnotherapy and a post-hypnotic suggestion was planted in Hobbs' psyche so that he would enter that house on Buller Street with a man he met at Jack's. That man has been searching for the Seven Seals for thousands of years, for that man is the human form of the Angel of Death. His angel name is Azazel, the same last name used by the owner of that house."

"But why did they need Hobbs," asked Aaron.

"Hobbs, without even realizing it, had been involved with the Angel of Death cult and the Black Arts. You see, Hobbs has served in many diplomatic posts for the USA. I am sure that you are familiar with Haiti, where during the reign of Papa Doc Duvalier rumours of him practicing the Dark Arts abounded. Papa Doc was assumed to have zombies in the basement of the Presidential Palace, and it just so happens that the most unusual case in regards to zombies occurred when Hobbs was there as assistant chargé d'affaires during the reign of Papa Doc's son, Jean-Claude Duvalier, who was in power from 1971 until 1986. It was there that Hobbs met a dashing man who

WHEN JESUS CAME TO LADYSMITH
TO BATTLE THE ANGEL OF DEATH

sported a Clark Cable type pencil moustache, and had an immense amount of charm. His name was Commodore Ralston Ray, who was also a young clerk at the Canadian embassy. He was; however, more than a clerk. You see, he was there also in search of the Seven Seals, which he assumed was being used by Papa Doc François Duvalier, and then by his son Jean Claude to give them power to summon and control what they called the un-dead, those who had died and been brought back to life - zombies. They used them to instil fear in the Haitian people, a people who are very backward and even today many still bow before the cult of the Duvalier's. Did the zombies really exist? Who knows?"

"But how about the involvement of Hobbs? How did this lead him here to Ladysmith," asked a bewildered Aaron.

"As I stated, Hobbs and Commodore Ray were in Haiti at the same time. It was there that Commodore Ray probably found out that Hobbs was susceptible to post hypnotic suggestion. In 1984 a very strange thing happened in Port-au-Prince, Haiti. Baby Doc Duvalier was growing fearful as it appeared his usefulness to the USA was growing tenuous. He feared they would overthrow him and install someone more compliant to their will. For that reason, he wanted to invoke the Rite of Judgement, a rite that called for a man to slay his brother; and thereby, release the full force of the Seven Seals, unleashing Armageddon. It just so happened that Hobbs had a brother who was working for the International Aid Society. And guess what? Hobbs' brother was killed in Port-au-Prince one night, killed in a very unusual manner."

Aaron, shaking his head in bewilderment that Jesus and Nichola had out sleuthed him and said, "So, don't tell me, according to the rites that must be performed to find the Seven Seals, an innocent victim has to be sacrificed through fratricide just as Cain slew Abel. That is what happened in Port-au-Prince, and, of course, the heart was removed from the chest by a scythe."

"Bingo!"

Still bewildered, Aaron said "But why has Hobbs not related this to us?"

"Why? Because he received a post-hypnotic suggestion to forget what happened to his brother. We asked him today if he had a brother. He replied that he did not, but we checked birth records in his hometown of Lockport, New York. His brother was born in 1952 in Lockport and died in 1984 in Port-Au-Prince – murdered. The culprit was never brought to justice, which was not uncommon in a place like Haiti in those days. Murder was a prevalent practice by both the public and the government."

WHEN JESUS CAME TO LADYSMITH
TO BATTLE THE ANGEL OF DEATH

"You are saying then that he killed his own brother, just as Edison killed his, but has blotted out the memory?"

Sighing, Nichola said "I am afraid so. There is no need to confront him with it. He is an old man, and is unaware of what he did. I say let sleeping dogs lie. Let the old man die in peace."

Still perplexed, Aaron asked, "But why involve Hobbs here and now. It makes no sense."

"Robert Edison's body was to be used in the Rite of Judgement ceremony no less than three times, two of which have already occurred. The body was preserved for those purposes through the use of a drug called Tetrodotoxin, also known as the zombie drug, an ancient concoction used in Haiti by voodoo practitioners. The preservation was necessary for the body to be used in the sacrificial rites three times as the devil is conjured to appear. He will, the coven hopes, appear when the third part of the ceremony is performed, and when the devil manifests himself he will point the way to the place where the seals can be found. We believe this action is set for tonight, but there will be no seals found, as I am fleeing right now, fleeing to where I can tell know one, a place where the seals will be safe. Now, where Hobbs enters the scene is what is most interesting. It all goes back to Haiti; where Commodore Ray had clandestinely hypnotized him and had him slay his own brother, then blot out any memory of doing it, even any memory of having a brother. In Haiti, it is my guess, along with Jesus, that Hobbs was used, as the slayer of his brother to represent the evil of fratricide. This made him a key figure in the Rites of Judgement and with him and Lloyd Edison both present, both of who committed fratricide, the power to call the devil will be increased, making it more likely he will appear."

Love is a sweet thing that floats like a butterfly
Over the nectar of a sweet flower in the spring.

Nichola arose and said with tears in her eyes, "I cannot reveal where I am going, but I shall always carry you in my heart, and, if by chance, I can trust someone else with my mission, I shall one day find you again. I promise."

As Jesus and Lynton stood outside looking inside, Aaron and Nichola embraced. The man who was once said to have a barbed wire soul stood with moistened eyes and watched as the woman he loved walked out with the Seven Seals under her right arm. She smiled at Jesus and Lynton, not saying a word, as the smile and knowing nod said it all. She turned to her right and walked up the street, never looking back.

Aaron came outside and stood fighting back tears, stoically watching his improbable lover, the woman who lit a fire he had long ago assumed had

WHEN JESUS CAME TO LADYSMITH
TO BATTLE THE ANGEL OF DEATH

been extinguished forever, moving gracefully with pride up the inclining street as if she was a lioness engineered by a higher power, a lioness in a jungle of concrete and steel that would protect her domain and never give in to despair. Still, she was tempered by a sense of loss, although claiming victory with the Seven Seals under her arm.

She had pride like Maya Angelou.
You can try destroying her with lies.
You can write her down in history,
But against evil she shall always rise.

She has determination and sassiness,
When the world is filled with gloom.
Why? Because she walks proudly
With tenacity, zip and zoom.

You will not see her broken,
With bowed head and lowered eyes.
She will fight back with persistence,
Because she hears humanity's cries.

You may think you have won.
You may sense victory with lies.
You cannot kill her with hatefulness,
For like the sun she will always rise.

Without any shame she shall rise.
Up from the past she shall rise.
Against evil she shall rise!
Stand in awe and watch her rise!

J. Wayne Frye   267

WHEN JESUS CAME TO LADYSMITH
TO BATTLE THE ANGEL OF DEATH

Jesus turned to Lynton, and as his eyes twinkled with sincerity, he said, "My dear Lynton, you have unparalleled, unmatched beauty and grace, but more importantly, you have an aura of kindness that brightens the lives of all lucky enough to bask in the warmth that flows from you like the bright rays of the sun on a cold December day. You light up a world of despicably sullen indifference with a commitment to truth and justice. I count myself lucky to have known you even for this short period of time. You will soon be but a memory, but a memory that will become a treasure to me, and dwell in a special please in my heart."

Turning to Aaron, Jesus said "My work here is done. Yours I do not envy, for you must tell a man of his crime, a crime that will haunt him. Maybe even destroy him. You, my friend, are the last of a dying breed, a man of integrity and righteousness, not the kind of false integrity and deceitful righteousness practiced by the hypocrites who wave about that black book of spurious deception called a Bible, but a man who knows the value of truth."

Neither Lynton nor Jesus could offer a reply as he gave them no time to do so. He turned and walked up the same street Nichola had stridden. You knew he was a man who carried on his shoulders the burdens of a world gone askew. He was a wanderer on a lonely path of heartache and lost hope.

WHEN JESUS CAME TO LADYSMITH
TO BATTLE THE ANGEL OF DEATH

He was born to be a wanderer,
Always rolling from here to there.
His bags are always packed.
He has never seen a sight
That didn't seem better looking back.

He was born to be a wanderer.
Settling can make him a prisoner,
And the world's evil can bake him dry,
But what really breaks his heart
Is people living with lie after lie.

He was born to be a wanderer,
Trying to lift the hopes and spirits
Of those whose dreams never come true.
He longs for a world where good triumphs,
But it never seems to no matter what he might do.

There are times when Aaron understood why his job was called the lonely profession. Why was it lonely? Simply because he bore the burdens of those who reach out for help, hoping that he would provide the answers that would ease their pain. Unfortunately, many times the pain is not diminished through an investigation, but is elevated to an almost unbearable level. Unfortunately, although Aaron was brave far beyond the norm, and as alluded to earlier, even referred to as "the man with a barbed wire soul," his compassion was so deep that he could feel the loneliness of his profession seeping from the cesspool of life that must be endured by so many.

J. Wayne Frye   269

WHEN JESUS CAME TO LADYSMITH
TO BATTLE THE ANGEL OF DEATH

Aaron contemplated telling Hobbs the truth, both truths. The one about how he wound up in that house would be easy, but how could he break the news about what he had done long ago in Haiti. He had plenty of practice giving people bad news, but just how do you tell a man he killed his own brother as part of an abominable ceremony performed to call up the devil from the dark pit and then he blotted the memory out? Aaron felt he might be a traitor to grief, watching and listening, even as he spoke the formal words of condolence and understanding, for the flicker of his eyelid, the tensing of hands and face muscles, for the unwise word that might perchance cause the dismay that would push Hobbs over the edge. He had to be very careful.

Lynton could sense Aaron's consternation. She knew that he had moved, as if by an unconscious act of will, into a world in which time was precisely measured, details obsessively noticed, senses preternaturally alerted to sound, smell, sight, even the smallest flick of an eyelid and the timbre of a voice no matter how soft was like a giant wave roaring assure on a lonely beach. She felt sorry for him, and as was usual with her kind hearted nature, she offered solace, as she reached down and took his hand. "I do not envy you my friend. You have seen a lover walk away, not because of anything you have done, but because she has a sense of duty to protect the world from evil. There are times bad luck comes, and then you wait to see what the universe and you can make of it, how you can make something good come of something so very awful. I can see nothing good coming from what you must do, and I am here by your side if you need me."

Aaron said, "How many times I have heard it recounted of your kindness I cannot count. You are proof that you can see more with your heart than your eyes. Eyes can tell you the result of what happened, never the reason, the intention, the deep emotions that swim below. It is only with the heart that you can see true pain, see the sadness that dwells beneath. Perhaps when the heart is our eyes, our eyes will finally show how important love is, and we can all, as humans, feel connected within and healed, able to walk with compassion. You elevate compassion to its finest form, Lynton."

They walked together toward the Dunsmuir Club, where they knew they would find Hobbs. They would not share what they knew with anyone but him, because they had decided to leave it up to him what to do with the knowledge they had gained. He could turn himself in, and probably never be convicted of a crime. Perhaps it was better to not tell him they both thought. A lack of knowledge might spare him a lifetime of self-recrimination. Yet, Aaron had a job to do, and he felt duty bound, as did Lynton, to lay all the cards on the table. It was the truly ethical thing to do, but sometimes ethics can be trumped by compassion.

Just as intelligence and complexity are different, so are wisdom and kindness. It is wise to be kind, but not to give so much to those that cause hurt and pain as to let them create new victims. Kindness must be tempered. It is both kind and wise to have the forethought to protect those who have done no wrong, and thus the kindness to the perpetrators of violence must be balanced against just how much damage that violence has caused. The purveyors of violence should receive care and justice as well as society can best afford, but not be given the freedom to hurt again. Should they be remorseful and maybe even proven cured of criminal maladies, is it possible that punishment is the only way to redemption? None of this invokes the idea of forgiveness; to this equation it is irrelevant. We can forgive and still require protection, and to provide such protection is wise. Being aware of his propensity for post-hypnotic suggestion, could Hobbs be rendered into a state where he would never again let such evil befall him?

As the two walked into the club archway, they were still contemplating what must be done. They suddenly turned, walked out without seeing Hobbs or anyone else. They did not even speak to each other. They instinctively knew what had to be done for their own piece of mind, as they moved toward that infernal house where wickedness had been called up from the dark pit where it incubated and grew.

Aaron, looking concerned, said to Lynton, "You need not do this. This is my job."

Lynton replied, "The devil doesn't come dressed in a red cape. He doesn't have pointed horns. He doesn't have hoofs for feet. He is wearing a well-tailored suit and has a meticulously groomed head of hair as he stands on a pair of Italian hand-made loafers with a pen in his hand to sign the papers that foreclose on your home. The devil is more than a scary nightmare. He is the real life corporate executive who is trying to figure out a way to raise profits by giving you a shoddy product that will wear out so you have to replace it with an even shoddier product. The devil is that politician with his hand out to his corporate controllers, as he takes an exorbitant government salary and accumulates parsimonious benefits while telling you to tighten your belt for the good of the country. So, the devil we are about to face is a puny comparison to the devil most people have to face every single day of their lives."

She took a deep breath and continued. "It is everybody's job to kick some devil worshipping butts once-in-awhile. The last time I kicked some of that type butt was in the Flats area of Cape Town, where evil had taken hold and my high heels from hell dealt a devastating blow for justice. Let's kick some devil worshipping butt. I am ready for action!"

These were two people not prone to trivialize the process of evil flourishing in a world where the few preyed on the many in pursuit of financial rewards. They knew evil flourished in its search for receptive minds. It whispered softly to the cadence of deception and invaded any person so damaged or disordered as to be unable to resist its siren call of power, vengeance and greed. They understood the process by which it was expressed, but were not so arrogant or so self-righteous as to think you can control it. Know thy enemy was their creed, and they knew the enemy was actually supported by finger-pointing Pharisees who waved the Bible while walking the crooked road of hypocrisy. Know evil's name and realize that its name is far too often – **you**!

These two denizens of righteousness, who were determined dispensers of justice, realized that evil was not just the devil but a world that lived in ignorance. If the Bible was true, God commanded his chosen people to destroy men simply for the crime of defending their native land. They were not allowed to spare trembling and white-haired aged people, nor dimpled babes clasped in mothers' arms. They were ordered to kill women, and to pierce, with the sword of war, the unborn child. God commanded the Hebrews to kill men and women, the fathers, sons and brothers, but to preserve the girls alive. Why were these maidens not also killed? Why were they spared? In the thirty-first chapter of Numbers, it is clearly spelled out that the maidens were given to the soldiers and the priests. Is there, in all the history of war, a more infamous thing than this? Is it possible that God permitted the violets of modesty that grow and shed their perfume in the maiden's heart to be trampled beneath the brutal feet of lust? If this was the order of a loving God, what, under the same circumstances, would have been the command of the devil? Could the devil do worse? Was this type abhorrent action not a war crime? Should God be in the dock of the World Court in The Hague for crimes against humanity?

Aaron and Lynton understood why this evil thing, this Angel of Death, hated men and women so much. He hated them because they were so like him, because the worst of him was mirrored in them. He was the source of all that was bad in men and women, but he had none of the greatness, and none of the grace of which human beings were capable, so only by corrupting them through their own inherent evil was he able to diminish his own pain, and thus his existence was made more tolerable. It was true that misery loved company.

As the two neared Buller Street, they noticed a winged thing streaking overhead, swiftly flying toward Roberts Street, where Jesus was putting his clothes in a trash bag he used for a suitcase, readying to depart Ladysmith, and they instantly knew why it was headed in that direction. They knew that Azazel, Commodore Ray and the Angel of Death were the same. Those three entities had descended upon Ladysmith to wreck havoc in search of the Seven Seals, but the seals, thanks to Jesus and Nichola, were on their way to a safe haven. Now, the Angel of Death had to leave and begin the search anew.

Suddenly, the pair heard a loud explosion on Buller Street. They ran in that direction, as they heard another explosion and saw huge plumes of smoke bellowing skyward above the surrounding buildings. They turned onto Buller and were greeted with soaring flames engulfing that house of vile abominations.

The lady next door was standing on her porch sporting a broad smile. Aaron and Lynton approached her, and she said, "Ain't it beautiful? Finally that devil's den of evil is gone. Haven't called the fire department yet, 'cause I want to make sure it can't be saved. Most beautiful fire I ever seen."

Aaron said, as sirens could be heard wailing in the background and people began to pour out of their homes and the streets filled with onlookers, "Well, if you had some marshmallows you could roast them."

WHEN JESUS CAME TO LADYSMITH
TO BATTLE THE ANGEL OF DEATH

Aaron took Lynton's hand and pulled her away. They walked toward First Street and Aaron said, "The evil has been staid for awhile. I see no need to burden Hobbs with what happened in Haiti. He is an old man with only a few years left. He has no memory of a crime that was instigated by an evil Angel of Death in the person of Commodore Ray. As the saying goes, let sleeping dogs lie.' I say we let 'um lie."

"Agreed," replied Lynton. "Go to Hobbs and give him my regards and well wishes. My dear husband will be home tonight. I shall go home, and prepare for his arrival and for his admonitions for once again getting involved in an adventure he will say I should have avoided. Come see us whenever you get the chance."

Aaron bade her a very fond farewell with a slight tinge of jealousy, because unlike him, she had someone to go home to, someone who brought great joy into her life, and all he had was a lonely bed in a lonely apartment in lower Manhattan's eastside.

As Lynton made her way to her car, she reflected on all that had ensued, and wondered if Jesus was confronting Commodore Ray at the Jenks' Boarding House, laying before him the fact that the seals were safe. And she also wondered about Nichola. She was a brave woman who put the safety of humanity before her love of Aaron.

Still, she felt deep sorrow for Aaron who had dealt with his share of sorrow over the years. He was indeed a man who walked a path of anguish and heartache too often in what he referred to as the lonely profession. She felt alone too, because Wayne had been gone for two weeks on his dreaded book tour, which she could not go on because of other committments. She got the slightest hint of smile as she thought that had she gone, she would have avoided all this trouble. Yet, as Wayne often said, "Trouble was her middle name." That was why he called her *his little headache.*

WHEN JESUS CAME TO LADYSMITH
TO BATTLE THE ANGEL OF DEATH

Epilogue
Grand Karma

Believe in light;
Believe in loneliness.
Believe in friends;
Believe in sorrow.
Believe in joy;
Believe in pain.
Believe in empathy,
Believe in frustration.
Believe in patience;
Believe in anger.
Believe in perspective;
Believe in indifference.
Above all, believe in love;
Because that offers hope.

J. Wayne Frye   279

WHEN JESUS CAME TO LADYSMITH
TO BATTLE THE ANGEL OF DEATH

Just as Lynton was walking toward her car at the far end of the town, Jesus was saying goodbye to the friends he had made at the Jenks' Boarding House. As he was preparing to leave, he glanced to the top of the stairs and saw Commodore Ray walking down with his suitcase. Joining Jesus, he said, "I think we have both concluded our business here. But I am sure we shall meet again."

Jesus replied, "The business of fighting evil is never finished for me. It is my fulltime job!"

Jesus, giving Mary Jenks a wink, walked outside, took a deep breath of fresh air and turned left to walk down the street toward town. The commodore came out, turned to his right and walked in the opposite direction.

Does the soaring eagle know what is in the pit?
Or wilt thou go ask the Mole:
"Can evil be put only on the devil's rod,
And love only put in a golden bowl?"

Wayne Borman was a grand friend of Wayne's who lived in a nearby town, and he had become a friend of Lynton's, too. His wife had died a couple of years ago, and, in order to assuage his loneliness, Wayne and Lynton had reached out to him and tried to elevate his spirits. In most people's lives, true friends can be counted on one hand. He was one of those friends in Wayne Frye's life, a person who could truly be depended on to give you a hand up when you were down, as he had done for Wayne so many times. Theirs was that kind of friendship that blooms in the centre of your heart; that kind of friendship that grows from the seed basking in the warm, moist soil growing into a vast tree with many towering branches reaching for the sky, a tree of enormity and grandeur, with the sheer brilliance and beauty that makes one ponder the magnificence of such a specimen. This was their friendship.

The two of them had forged a unique bond based on a severe mutual dislike of greed that permeated all the earth's societies and made the world an untenable place for the many that were compelled to serve the interests of the few. Their mutual disdain for capitalism with all its faults that rewarded the privileged at the expense of working men and women had made them compatriots in the battle for justice in a world where it was in short supply. They were two ageing warriors who had never surrendered their belief that a true revolution of the downtrodden and forgotten was possible.

Borman had also developed immediate rapport with Lynton, as he could see in her an individual with great depth of character. So, there friendship blossomed into genuine respect.

As he was driving through Ladysmith, he saw her walking and pulled over. Surprised and overjoyed, she came to the passenger side door, opened it and slid in saying, "How wonderful to see you. It has been far too long."

"Yes, it has been. Have you had lunch yet?" asked Wayne.

"No, and there is no one I would rather have it with than you, especially if you are paying."

They shared a mutually boisterous laugh and had a leisurely lunch at Jack's, and then, just as they were about to leave, Wayne said with a quizzical manner, "I have a question for you. Did you ever hear of a man named Lloyd Edison, who lives in Victoria? He is a strange character I had a run in with long ago, and I just saw him being arrested on First Avenue.

Smiling with the knowledge that Edison had obviously been finally tied to the extremely gruesome murder of his brother and was now going to pay for his crime, Lynton said, "My guess is you just witnessed grand karma. Do I know him? If you only knew," replied Lynton. "Why?"

Shaking his head, Wayne replied, "Well………"